the Vampire Diaries

Stefan's Diaries

volume six
THE COMPELLED

Based on the novels by

L. J. SMITH

and the TV series developed by
Kevin Williamson and Julie Plec

Hodder
Children's
Books

A division of Hachette Children's Books

Text copyright © 2012 by Alloy Entertainment and L.J. Smith

First published in the USA in 2012 by
HarperTeen, an imprint of HarperCollins Publishers

This edition published in Great Britain in 2012
by Hodder Children's Books

1

ISBN: 978 1 444 91000 1

Typeset in Berkeley by Avon DataSet Ltd,
Bidford on Avon, Warwickshire

Printed and bound in Great Britain by
Clays Ltd, St Ives plc

The paper and board used in this paperback by Hodder Children's Books are natural recyclable products made from wood grown in sustainable forests. The manufacturing processes conform to the environmental regulations of the country of origin.

Hodder Children's Books
a division of Hachette Children's Books
338 Euston Road, London NW1 3BH
An Hachette UK Company
www.hachette.co.uk

PREFACE

The only thing in the world that's constant is war. It was an aphorism murmured in the sticky summer of 1864 as the Civil War tore America apart – and it was a truth that had only become more evident in my twenty years as a vampire. Every time I picked up the paper, there were stories of humans fighting humans: brawls on the streets of San Francisco, uprisings in India, insurrections all over Europe. And once blood had been shed and graves marked, they'd start all over again.

But the war that my brother, Damon, and I were fighting against the evil vampire Samuel Mortimer was far different. It was a battle without limits. After all, human soldiers instinctively fear death. As vampires, we'd already conquered it. What we feared was the reign of terror Samuel would surely inflict upon London if he won. Evil would run rampant.

To the citizens of London, Samuel Mortimer was a member of the city's political elite. But we knew his true nature: he was a fiendish vampire, one we'd been trying to destroy for weeks. Not only had he fed on the blood of innocent women and tried to kill me, he had framed my brother as Jack the Ripper – a now infamous name for the deranged killer responsible for the Whitechapel murders, which Samuel himself was committing.

He'd also been one of Katherine's lovers. Katherine – the vampire who'd seduced Damon and me and fanned the flames of discord between us two decades ago – had turned us into the creatures we now were. Samuel was convinced we'd killed his love, and he wanted revenge. It didn't matter that Damon and I hadn't been the ones to trap and burn her in the church back in Mystic Falls. He would never believe we'd tried to save her. Samuel needed someone to pay for her death, and he'd chosen us. No matter what, it seemed neither decades nor miles nor oceans could separate me from Katherine's legacy.

But this time it was different. Her memory hadn't divided my brother and me. Instead, it had united us against Samuel. We'd managed to kill his brother, Henry, before the battle had taken a terrible turn, but Samuel had captured Damon. I knew he could kill him in a second if he wanted to. Right now, the only thing keeping Damon from death was Samuel's penchant for torture and sadistic games. I had to rescue Damon from his suffering before Samuel tired of him.

I wasn't afraid to die. But, as odd as it was after our years of fighting, I was afraid to live in a world without Damon. My brother was callous, rude and destructive. And yet he had saved me on more than one occasion during our time in London. He was the one I could count on when no one else could be trusted. He was all I had.

After all, we were bound by blood. And if I'd learned anything from my time as a vampire, it was that blood was life. Without Damon, my life force would ebb. Now I had to do everything in my power to get him back . . .

CHAPTER 1

There was a moment after Samuel dragged Damon away when it seemed as though my spirit had left my body. It was how I'd felt when a bullet from my father's gun had pierced my chest all those years ago in Mystic Falls: a split second of agony, followed by a blankness that radiated from the very core of my being.

But I wasn't dead. And I wouldn't let Samuel escape with Damon. Once I'd made sure Cora was all right, I took a deep breath and catapulted my body out of the window of the Magdalene Asylum. Glass shattered around me and a shard pierced my cheek. Blood ran down my skin. I didn't care.

'Damon!' I yelled. The Asylum was empty – no one would hear me. All the residents, nuns and priests were at a midnight church service, which had been convenient for Damon and me when we set our trap for Samuel.

We'd had weapons. We'd had plans. We'd had the

element of surprise. And still we'd fallen short. It was as if Samuel had purposely allowed us to get closer and closer, only to outwit us — just like his alter ego Jack the Ripper had done with the Metropolitan Police when he sent them on a cat-and-mouse chase through London.

I ran through the city streets at vampire speed, trying to listen for shouts, scuffles, even laboured breathing — anything that would lead me to my brother. I knew it was useless, but I had to do something. After all, Damon had saved me from Samuel. He deserved the same from me.

I ran through Dutfield Park, the overgrown square where Damon and I had first realised we were being hunted. It would be poetic justice for Samuel to kill him here, beneath the stone wall where he'd written a chilling message in blood to let us know he would have his revenge. But I noticed nothing amiss. The only sounds were the scampering of squirrels in the undergrowth and the whistling of the wind through barren trees.

I ran to the highest point of the park and glanced around in all directions: the elegant dome of St Paul's Cathedral, the ominous, dark ribbon of the Thames snaking through the city, the run-down buildings crowding the park. Damon could be anywhere.

He could already be dead.

I jammed my hands in my pockets and turned round,

slowly walking back to the Asylum. I needed to get Cora; together, we'd come up with something. It was what we'd been doing for the past several weeks: trailing Samuel, thinking we'd captured him, and then finding ourselves in a worse situation than ever.

Even before I reached the gates of the Asylum, I could hear a low-pitched moan: Cora. My heart twisted in sorrow thinking of her. I wasn't the only one missing a family member. Samuel had taken her sister, Violet, and turned her into a vampire. Violet had attacked her own sister. Of course Cora was mourning.

I entered the Asylum through the window I'd broken. The smell of Henry's burning flesh still clung to the room. There was blood pooled on the floor and spattered across the walls, as though the subterranean office had become an impromptu butcher's shop. Which, I suppose, it had.

Standing in the corner, Cora moaned again, her hand clasped to her mouth. She was an innocent girl caught in an increasingly tangled web of evil and despair. Only a fortnight ago, Samuel had turned Violet into a vampire. Ever since then, Cora had been doing whatever she could to try to save her, including infiltrating the Magdalene Asylum, of which Samuel was a well-known benefactor. As soon as she'd realised Samuel was affiliated with the Asylum, she'd volunteered to pose as a destitute girl seeking salvation within its doors. It was she who'd found out that Samuel was using the Asylum residents as his own personal blood supply. And it was she who'd helped set up a trap to snare Samuel. We had hoped to get closer to him, to discover his weaknesses, anything that could help us understand his relentless vendetta against us. Because the Ripper murders weren't committed for the blood. As vampires, we could kill quickly and cleanly – but we didn't need to murder to obtain sustenance. Samuel, especially, didn't: as a benefactor to the Magdalene Asylum, he was able to drink his fill from its residents whenever he liked, compelling them to offer their necks to him and then forget all about the encounter. And yet he was intent on brutally slaying and slicing open victims on the streets of Whitechapel, all with the goal of framing Damon as a killer. His motivation could be summed up in one terrible name: Katherine.

At one point, the name had made my heart race. Now it made it clench in dread. Katherine meant Samuel, and Samuel meant destruction. And the only question was, when would he stop? When Damon was dead? When I was dead? In the process of our investigation, we'd lost Damon and witnessed Violet's transformation into a soulless, cold-blooded killer. Not only had she fought brutally against Damon and me moments earlier, but she'd hurt – and worse, fed on – Cora. I could only imagine the despair and confusion Cora was feeling as she stood in the corner.

But I couldn't dwell on what had happened. I needed to think of the future – and I needed to save Damon.

'We can't stay here. Let's go home.' Our destination was the Underground tunnel where we'd spent our nights for the last week.

Cora nodded. A flicker of concern crossed her eyes as she noticed the cut on my cheek.

'You're bleeding,' she said.

'I'm fine,' I said roughly, wiping the blood away with my hand. It was just like Cora to be worried about my discomfort when *she* was struggling with so much.

'Let me help you.' She reached into the sleeve of her dress and pulled out a handkerchief. She tenderly rubbed it against my skin. 'I'm worried about you, Stefan. You have to take care of yourself, because . . .' She trailed off, but I knew what she was thinking. *Because at this point, you're all I have.* I nodded, knowing there wasn't much else she or I could say.

I boosted her up so she could climb through the Asylum window, and together we slowly trudged westward to our temporary home.

Above us, clouds and mist obscured any stars and the streets were practically empty. People were terrified of the Ripper, and the eerie wind whistling through the alleys added to the evil tone of the evening. The only heartbeat I could hear was Cora's, but I knew from the papers that policemen were hiding in every shadowy alley, on the lookout for the Ripper.

Of course, the police presence was useless. While they were shivering on the streets, on guard for the Ripper's next attack, the murderer was preoccupied with a prime distraction: plotting to torture my brother.

At least, I hoped he was still plotting rather than already tormenting Damon. Was my brother even now crying out in agony? Or had Samuel simply staked him and thrown his lifeless body in the Thames? Tortured or killed? It was a lose–lose situation, but I found myself wishing Samuel's sadistic nature had won out. While it would prolong Damon's pain, it gave us a chance of rescuing him, boosting our slim odds.

Cora stumbled and I reached out to steady her. We were almost home. I paused to make sure we hadn't been followed, but no one was chasing us. In fact, no one seemed to be here at all, perhaps put off by the signs that surrounded the work area above the tunnel, all clearly stating that trespassing was strictly prohibited by the Metropolitan Police.

I jumped down into the tunnel, unfazed by the drop. That was one of the advantages of being a vampire: my innate agility ensured I'd land on my feet.

I helped Cora down, and the two of us faced each other. Despite the darkness, I could see everything, from the packed dirt walls to the pebbles scattered on the ground. Meanwhile, Cora blinked several times, her eyes adjusting to the lack of light.

Suddenly, a creature darted past our feet. It was a rat, almost the size of a small cat. Instead of scrambling away in surprise, Cora grabbed a large stone from the tunnel floor and threw it at the creature. The scuffling stopped.

'You need to eat,' she urged.

'Thank you.' I reached down, grabbed the still-warm carcass and placed my mouth to its fur, piercing the thin skin with my fangs. The whole time, I was aware of Cora's unflinching gaze. But what did it matter? It wasn't as though my drinking blood was a surprise to her. She'd seen me bare my fangs to feed, and she'd seen me battle Henry and Samuel. I felt the rat's blood calm my body as it ran through my veins.

Once I'd drunk all I could, I threw the carcass to the ground, wiped my mouth with the back of my hand and smiled briefly at Cora. Our friendship was unlike any I'd ever experienced with a human since becoming a vampire. Even when Callie had discovered my identity back in New Orleans, I had never fed in front of her. I had concealed my fangs and masked my yearnings, wanting her only to see the best in me. But Cora was different.

'Was that enough?' she asked, sliding into a seated position and crossing her legs under her grey dress, now spattered with dirt and blood. Dark shadows surrounded her eyes and the smudges of grime on her cheeks blended with the smattering of freckles on her skin. Her teeth were chattering. A cold snap had hit London in the past few days, and it was especially frigid in the tunnel, where the walls were beaded with condensation, and a misty grey fog swirled around the darkness.

'It was, thank you. How are you?' I asked, feeling stupid as soon as the words escaped my lips. How was she? She was in the tunnel of an all-but-abandoned construction site. She'd just killed a rat and watched as it was drained of its blood. She'd been betrayed by her vampire sister. She'd witnessed vampires torturing one another, seen a body burned to ashes. And although she did so willingly, she'd been used as a pawn in our war against Samuel. But he'd escaped, and had brutally killed two of her friends, then left their corpses in Mitre Square. How did I expect her to feel?

'I'm alive,' Cora said. 'I believe that counts for something.' She attempted a laugh, but it came out as a sputtering cough. I patted her on the back and was surprised when she leaned in and gave me a hug.

'I'm sorry I put you in danger,' I said hollowly. 'I should

have known that we couldn't reason with Violet. I should never have brought you to see her.' We'd gone to see Ephraim, a witch, and had him cast a locator spell to help us find Violet and persuade her to leave Samuel. But when we'd found her, she hadn't listened to anything we'd said and had kidnapped Cora, which is how she'd ended up back at the Asylum the same day Damon and I had sneaked in to ambush Samuel.

'You wouldn't have been able to keep me away from Violet,' Cora said firmly. 'You told me she wouldn't be the same. But deep down, I believed she'd still be my sister. Now I know I was wrong.' She shuddered. I nodded, sad that my prediction had been true.

'I was so *stupid*,' she said, her face twisting in anger. 'I thought I could get through to her. I thought she could change. But there was nothing of Violet left in her. She *fed* on me, Stefan. Then she brought me to the Asylum and asked that groundskeeper, Seaver, to lock me in that room. I tried to escape, but Seaver started chanting and all of a sudden, I was completely trapped.' Her lower lip wobbled as tears spilled down her cheeks. She wiped them away with the back of her hand and set her mouth in a firm line.

'He must have used some sort of spell,' I said slowly. I remembered how small and helpless Cora had looked in that room in the Magdalene Asylum. She must have been terrified.

13

'We need to see Ephraim,' I decided. The only thing I knew for certain was that if Samuel had witches under his control, we'd need a way to counter their spells.

'No!' Cora yelled. 'Not Ephraim. I had a bad feeling about him. His locator spell may have taken us to Violet, but what if that was a trap he set up with Samuel? What if he's been working for Samuel all along? We know Ephraim used to do jobs for the highest bidder – who's to say he ever stopped? We can't trust him,' she said, setting her jaw. 'We need to come up with another plan.'

'Well, we need *someone* on our side who can perform magic. Otherwise, Samuel will always have that advantage over us,' I said. I stood up and paced back and forth, willing my mind to come up with a clever way to ensnare Samuel and free my brother. But I still felt weak and shaky and utterly unable to concentrate. The rat's blood had only taken the edge off my hunger.

'I think you should drink real blood,' Cora said quietly, as if she could read my mind. 'Like your brother. Like Samuel. It would make you strong enough to fight him, right? It would make the fight even, like you said.' Her eyes glittered like diamonds in the darkness.

'I can't!' I exploded in frustration, unleashing all the tension I'd been holding in. My voice echoed off the walls of the tunnel, sending rodents skittering to unknown hiding spots. A few nights earlier, I would have heard the far-off moans and heartbeats of other tunnel dwellers. Tonight, there were none, and I was glad they'd moved on. The sound of blood rushing against veins would be far too tempting. I took a steadying breath. 'I can't control myself,' I continued more calmly. 'When Damon feeds, he's smarter and faster. When I feed, all I want is more blood. I can't think logically or rationally. All I can think of is how I'll hunt my next meal. I'm a beast on blood, Cora.'

She opened her mouth as if to say something, then thought better of it. 'All right. But, Stefan,' she said, grabbing my wrist in a surprisingly strong grip, 'this is war, and I won't have you lose on principle.'

'What do you mean?' I tugged my wrist away gently and peered at her. 'It's more than principle – it's survival. I don't drink human blood.'

'I know you don't. All I meant was that I'll do whatever it takes to stop Samuel from killing more innocent people. And I hope you'll do the same. Maybe drinking human blood would be different for you now. Maybe you could *try*.'

'I can't,' I said firmly. 'You don't know what blood does to me. And I don't want you to find out.'

Cora looked at me indignantly, but I didn't want to pursue the subject any further. 'We should get some sleep,' I said. I settled on the hard ground. I heard her shaky breathing, but I couldn't tell if she was shivering or crying. I didn't ask.

I closed my eyes and pressed my hand to my forehead, a gesture that did nothing to ease the relentless pounding in my skull. Cora's suggestion echoed in my mind: *Drink human blood.*

Could I? I hadn't in twenty years, not since I was in New Orleans, where I'd sometimes drunk the blood of four, five, ten humans a day with little thought to the consequences. I often dreamed of it, the moment when I was bent over a victim, smelling the rushing liquid iron, knowing it was about to run down my throat. Sometimes the liquid was bitter, like strong, black coffee. Sometimes it was sweet, with traces of honey and oranges. It used to be a private, perverse game of mine: to guess the taste before the blood touched my tongue. But no matter what the flavour, the result was the same: with human blood in me, I was stronger, faster.

And ruthless.

In a way, Cora was right. In the short term, blood could be the fuel to power me to rescue Damon. But in the long run, it would destroy me. And as much as I needed to save Damon, I needed to save myself, too.

I reached into the darkness and allowed my hand to graze her slim fingers. She took it and gently squeezed.

'I know you'll find a way to save Damon,' she said, '. . . with or without blood.'

It was meant to be reassuring, but I knew from the hesitancy in her voice that she was simply trying to make me feel better. She didn't really believe it – which only made me feel worse.

I turned to face her.

'I promise, if I need to drink blood, I will. You have my word.'

Relief flickered in her large eyes. 'Thank you,' she said.

I didn't fall asleep for a long time after that. I could sense from Cora's slow, deep breathing that the evening of terror had taken its toll. She was resting, exhausted, her face in calm repose. Meanwhile, my brain was reeling.

Damon, I whispered into the darkness.

Nothing.

CHAPTER 2

The next day I left the tunnel, telling Cora I needed to do some errands. She didn't offer to join me, and I wondered if she thought I was off to hunt human blood. If so, I let her believe it. But instead, all I did was joylessly kill a squirrel, feeling weak even as the blood hit my tongue. Human blood would make me feel sharp, alive. This only made me feel more despair.

Darkness had fallen when I returned to the tunnel. Cora climbed out to join me, and the two of us headed towards the Asylum. We knew Samuel often stopped there at the end of the day. If we could catch a glimpse of him as he exited, then follow him, we hoped he'd lead us to Damon. We were armed with stakes, but they provided minimal comfort. My stake was jammed in the leg of my boot and poked my skin every few steps. It didn't make me feel any safer. At this point, stakes were as commonplace to us as guns were to hunters heading into the woods. But having a gun didn't guarantee a hunter couldn't be killed.

The crisp autumn air smelled like burning leaves, and, unlike the East End, this part of town was filled with well-dressed men and women, strolling from dining clubs to the theatre to their fancy hotels. I didn't mind the crowds. Having to navigate through the masses and around horse-drawn carriages took my mind off the task at hand.

Gradually, the crowds thinned out and the smell of illicit fires made with newspaper kindling replaced the aroma of roasted chestnuts. The streets were empty, but the slums surrounding them were full, and I could sense eyes watching us suspiciously behind plateglass windows as we walked up Whitechapel High Street, the neighbourhood's main thoroughfare. From there, we turned onto Crispin Street and soon arrived at the Magdalene Asylum. The stone edifice towered, churchlike, over the now-empty Spitalfields Market. Cora's attention was focused on the padlock on the heavy iron gates of the building. The only sign that anyone inhabited the Asylum was a lone candle flickering in an upper window. It was only a little past eight o'clock but, unlike the rest of London, the street and building were as quiet as a tomb. It was, after all, only two blocks away from Mitre Square, the location of Jack the Ripper's most recent kills. Ever since then, the Whitechapel Vigilance Committee had urged residents of the East End to stay indoors. Clearly, they were taking the request seriously.

'I hope they're all right,' Cora said quietly, and I knew she was thinking of the girls she'd met when she'd infiltrated the Asylum. All young and down on their luck, they'd seen the organisation as a chance to get back on their feet. When they'd entered the Asylum, how could they possibly have known their blood would be used to feed monsters or that their benefactor would hand-pick them to be slain on the streets?

Behind us I heard the sound of leaves crunching. I turned, ready to face whatever new danger was heading our way, but it was only a watchman, swinging his nightstick in one hand and holding a lantern in the other.

Don't come over here, I willed, focusing my Power on him. He moved towards me, and for half a second our eyes locked. *Turn. Go back where you came from.* He paused, but didn't shine the light our way. Instead, he pivoted on his heel and walked back in the opposite direction.

'Did something happen?' Cora whispered sharply as she noticed my cocked head.

'Shh!' I motioned for her to be quiet until the footfalls faded. She didn't have the same ultra-honed senses I had and was oblivious to our near miss.

Before I could explain what I'd seen, the front door of the Asylum opened and Samuel strode out into the darkness, an attaché case under his arm and a silk top hat on his head. I stiffened as Cora grabbed my arm. I pulled her up the street behind a hedgerow, but Samuel didn't look towards us. To anyone passing him on the street, he was simply the future London councillor, out doing charity work for the poor. They would think him admirable, I reflected in disgust. He turned down the flint path towards the kerb and up the street, in the direction of the barren Spitalfields Market. As soon as he did, a coach veered towards him. Clearly, the driver was confident he could collect a generous fare from this well-dressed man.

'Here, sir! Happy to take you wherever you want!' the driver called across the square. Samuel nodded once, then hopped into the cab.

'Let's go,' I hissed to Cora, grabbing her arm and breaking into a run. Together we sprinted behind the coach as it clopped its way past the stalls surrounding the seedy market, heading deeper into Whitechapel. I was ten feet away, then five, and was about to catch up when I realised Cora was no longer on my arm.

I turned around and saw her doubled over, her hands on her knees, in front of the Lamb and Sickle public house. She had attracted the attention of a few patrons lurking in the doorway, who had stopped their round of singing to gape at her.

'I'm sorry. I just can't run any more,' she panted, her face red and slicked with sweat. 'You go on ahead.'

'No need to run, girl,' one man said as he lecherously stumbled towards her. 'You can relax in my arms.'

I turned to him and bared my fangs menacingly. He let go of Cora and backed away, his face white with fright.

'All right, no need to get nasty. Just having a bit of fun,' he said slowly, holding up his hands and walking away.

'Go on! I'll meet you later. I know the barman here. He'll take care of me. I'll be fine,' Cora urged with the same fierceness I'd seen last night.

'Are you sure?' I didn't want to leave her, but I couldn't lose Samuel. I glanced around. The Ten Bells was nearby. Cora did know the area, and she had a stake hidden in the folds of her skirt. I knew as well as she did that a stake would also do a perfectly fine job incapacitating a human threat. Still . . .

'Yes!' she hissed. 'I'll meet you back at the tunnel.'

I nodded and surged ahead at vampire speed, but the busy street beyond the market was crowded with coaches, and I no longer knew which one held Samuel.

I was about to cut my losses and head back to the pub to collect Cora when I spotted a figure stealing down a dark alley. I narrowed my eyes. The form was moving far more quickly than any human. Samuel. And worse, he was carrying a girl in his arms. The girl was clawing at his shoulder, forcing him to stop and adjust his hold every few feet. I couldn't believe she was still conscious. Many of Samuel's victims fainted from fright, or were killed immediately. But now he seemed to be taking care not to jostle the girl, holding her as carefully as a wolf would bring its prey back to the pack.

My heart clenched and I broke into a run when I realised he was heading for the warehouses near the Thames. I hadn't been there since the terrible night when Samuel had turned Violet into a vampire. Why was he taking a human girl there now? He had Damon; he didn't need to frame him for any more Jack the Ripper murders. He had a steady supply of blood from the girls in the Asylum. So what could he possibly want with *this* girl?

I followed the streak of Samuel's shadow along the brick buildings that led to the pier, but soon lost his trail. Further down the pier I could hear the sound of bottles breaking, but I knew that wasn't Samuel. The piers were lawless after dark, filled with lost souls – syphilitic soldiers, pickpockets and gamblers desperate to make money by any means necessary – people who couldn't even scrape together the few coins required to stay in a lodging house.

I cocked my head, trying to catch the scent of blood or the sounds of terrified, uneven breathing when I sensed someone close by. I turned. It was a toothless drunk, his breath sour with the stench of whisky. A knife shone in his hand.

'New boy,' he leered, pulling back the knife as though ready to plunge it into my abdomen.

I lunged towards him, pushing him onto his back. His knife clattered on the dock next to him. I set my boot down on his chest and leaned in close.

'Don't,' I hissed, as I felt my fangs growing from behind my gums. This was blood for the taking. I could drink, and be ready to face Samuel as a true vampire.

I was about to take a delicious, forbidden sip when I heard a sound. I whirled round. But it wasn't the girl, or Samuel. It was only two more drunks, leaning against each other for support.

I roughly kicked the man. 'Get up and run away,' I snarled.

He sprang to his feet and raced down the pier. I shoved the knife in my boot and angrily kicked a spray of rocks into the Thames. They landed with uneven splashes.

And then I heard it: a sound so faint I thought it was my imagination. One whimper, then another, from a warehouse several hundred yards away from where I stood. I rushed towards the building and found Samuel crouched against the wall, half obscured behind several discarded canvas ship sails. I pressed my back against the weathered wooden slats of the warehouse, priming my Power and readying myself to pounce, when I realised that the girl wasn't the one letting out the strangled sobs.

It was *Samuel*.

His mouth hung open in an expression of agony. His victim, meanwhile, was propped on her elbows, gazing intently into his face. Her lips were moving, but no sound was coming out of them. The girl was no older than eighteen or nineteen, with wild brown hair matted around her head. Whatever incantation she was using had momentarily incapacitated her assaulter, but before I could react, Samuel regained the upper hand and lunged, his teeth bared and glittering in the moonlight, using his brute force to throw her against the brick wall of the warehouse. Her head hit the wall with a sickening thud and she slumped to the ground in a heap.

Smiling, he pulled a long silver dagger from a pocket in his waistcoat, and I realised that he wasn't going to drink her blood. He was going to mutilate her the same way he'd defiled Jack the Ripper's other victims. He was going to slice open her chest.

In that instant, I yanked the stake out of my boot and

shoved it between his shoulder blades as hard as I could. Samuel fell forward onto the girl, then tumbled onto his side on the dock. Blood soaked through his coat. The girl sprang up and darted to the other side of the warehouse.

My hands trembled. I'd staked Samuel. And if I staked him through the heart, it would all be over. But it wasn't that easy. I needed him alive until he could take me to Damon.

He began to struggle to his feet, the wooden stake jutting unevenly from his back. I lunged forward to restrain his hands, but he spun away from me before I could reach him.

'These attempts are getting tiresome,' he hissed as he yanked the stake from his flesh and threw it onto the dock. I dived for it just as a police whistle sounded. The subsequent clattering of footsteps caused us both to freeze.

'Commotion at the warehouse!' cried a foghorn-like voice from the top of the pier.

Samuel stole off into the shadows as three police officers rounded the corner. Instead of following him, I calmly walked out of the alley, humming the song I'd heard the drunk singing outside the Lamb and Sickle as though I, too, was just a common vagrant.

'What's the trouble?' one red-faced officer wheezed as he valiantly tried to catch his breath. A taller policeman with a moustache appraised me suspiciously. I wondered where the girl had gone and whether she was in danger of Samuel doubling back for her.

'There is no trouble, sir,' I said, rising to my full height. 'Just having a bit of fun.' I wavered from one foot to the other as I said it, pretending I was a whisky-addled fool. I clenched my jaw, talking through my teeth to conceal my fangs, which always emerged when I was antsy.

The policeman glanced around, and I was thankful there were no gas lamps on the pier and he couldn't see the bloodstains on my clothes.

The sound of a bottle breaking further down the pier startled him. He turned his head sharply over his shoulder. From the shouts and glass shattering, it was clear a true brawl was brewing.

'I ain't got time to deal with you,' he said. 'Now, see you get into a lodging house. Make any more noise tonight, and you'll be arrested. Is that clear?' he asked.

'Yes, sir.' I nodded.

'Good.' The policeman hurried off to the scuffle while his short, red-faced partner struggled to keep up. As their footsteps faded, I realised I could hear the faint *ba-da-bump, ba-da-bump* of the mysterious girl's terrified heartbeat.

The moon filtered through the mist, casting an eerie green glow on the slippery dock, now tinged red with Samuel's blood. The *ba-da-bump, ba-da-bump* got louder and louder as I headed towards where I'd last seen the girl.

'Don't get any closer!' The voice sounded weak. I remembered the terrible crack, loud as a thunderbolt, when her skull hit the brick wall. She was crouched behind a crate in an alley next to the warehouse.

'Are you all right?' I asked, kneeling down so I was at eye level with her.

'I don't know.' She hesitantly pushed the crate away. Her eyes were catlike, the pupils more like keyholes than circles. I glanced away, nervous by how entranced I was by their unusual shape, only to see a slow but steady trickle of blood run from her temple and into her hair. 'I think he meant to kill me,' she said shakily.

'You're all right now,' I said in a soothing voice. 'Do you know why he was after you?'

The girl laughed, one short bark. 'Well, it wasn't because he liked me, I can tell you that much. No. When a vampire sets after you, you don't ask why.'

I rocked back on my heels in surprise. 'You knew he was a vampire?'

'Yes. And so are you,' she said. 'But you saved me. Why?'

'Why wouldn't I? Do you know who that man was?'

The girl shrugged. 'I knew he wanted to kill me, so we never got round to making formal introductions. I was just minding my own business and then—' She shuddered.

'You're safe now. I don't drink human blood. I only want to protect you.'

The girl's eyes blazed into mine, her pupils widening and contracting. And then, after a long moment, she nodded.

'Thank you for being honest,' she said. 'I'm Mary Jane. And I suppose you can tell that I'm more than I seem. You saw one of my tricks. I only wish it had worked better,' she added ruefully. She clearly knew how to control her power. But was she a witch? Or some other creature of darkness I'd never encountered? I leaned in, hoping to hear more about her trick. How had she pushed Samuel back?

Instead, she took a deep breath and said, 'So, who are *you*, vampire?'

But before I could respond, she fainted, hitting the dock with a muffled thud.

CHAPTER 3

Not knowing what else to do, I grabbed the unconscious girl and made my way back to the tunnel, staying in the shadows to avoid any suspicious glances. As expected, everyone on the pier was too involved in their own miseries to notice me, or the girl breathing shallowly in my arms.

When I finally managed to snake my way down to our makeshift camp, I was relieved to see Cora lying peacefully next to a small fire.

'Cora,' I said.

She started awake, her eyes widening as she took in the figure in my arms.

'Is that Damon? Is he dead?' Her voice was tinged with hysteria.

'No! No, it's not Damon,' I said hurriedly, trying to assuage her fears. 'It's a girl Samuel attacked. I got there before he could kill her.' I slowly placed the girl on the ground. Instinctively, she curled her small body towards the fire.

'He was trying to kill her?' Cora asked, wrinkling her nose. 'But I don't understand. He's already framed Damon. And he has all the blood he could want.'

'I know,' I said. Briefly, I tried to explain what I'd seen. The odd words Mary Jane had been muttering to keep Samuel away. The way Samuel seemed intent on killing her with a knife, rather than his fangs. The fact she'd known we were both vampires. And that she'd known I wasn't lying when I'd said I wouldn't hurt her.

The fire had burned down to its last embers, casting a flickering orange glow on Cora's face.

'I think you were right. We need to talk to Ephraim,' she said in resignation.

I nodded in agreement, unable to tear my eyes from the sleeping girl. Was *she* a witch? An image of Margaret Sutherland swam into my mind. Margaret, sister of Bridget, the girl I'd married in New York, was a witch. She had always known when someone was lying. In fact, that trait had once saved Damon and me: when Margaret came home to find her family brutally slaughtered, she'd been the only person who believed we hadn't killed them. For my sake, I hoped this girl had the same skill.

'What can I do to help?' Cora asked, gently tucking a

frayed flannel blanket around Mary Jane's thin shoulders.

'We'll see Ephraim at midnight tomorrow. There's nothing we can do in the meantime.'

Cora nodded and settled back into her pile of blankets, turning to face the wall. I'm not sure how long I sat, silently keeping watch. *Like Samuel would just burst in*, I thought. If he wanted to, he could. But he wouldn't. Here, in the dank tunnel, I felt safe. It was only out there – where Damon was right now – that was the problem.

I contemplated building up the fire, but didn't. Eventually, the sound of the girls' even inhalations and exhalations lulled me into a daze.

But I was startled out of my stupor when I heard the rustlings of Mary Jane coming round.

'Where am I?' she asked in a panic. The quaver in her voice hurt my heart.

'You're safe,' I said, trying to calm her. 'You fainted. I brought you here to protect you from Samuel. I saved you, remember?'

The girl nodded, relaxing. 'You're the vampire.'

'And you're a witch.'

'That I am,' she said softly. 'I'm Mary Jane Kelly. And you, vampire?' she asked pointedly.

'Stefan . . .' I paused. I was never sure whether to give my full name. But it didn't matter. She knew I was a vampire.

She knew when I was telling the truth. 'I'm Stefan Salvatore. And this is Cora Burns. She's human,' I added, gesturing to Cora, who had awoken at the noise.

'It's nice to meet you,' Cora said. 'Stefan, can you start the fire?'

'Of course,' I said quickly, grabbing a match from the cold, wet earth and hoping it wasn't too damp to light.

'A fire?' Mary Jane asked. 'I can do that.' She closed her eyes. '*Incendia*.'

Immediately, a fire crackled in the pit, casting ghostly shadows on the earthen walls. Cora's eyes widened in surprise. Despite everything, a glimmer of a smile crossed Mary Jane's face. It was clear she was pleased with her work.

'Can you tell me what you did to hold him back?' I asked, once we were all situated around the fire. 'It's important that we know. Because Samuel – the vampire who tried to kill you – has captured my brother.'

'Unfortunately, I'm much better at starting fires than staving off vampires,' Mary Jane said wryly. 'And warding off vampires isn't exactly a skill I'd like more practice in.'

'But you did *something*. He was trying to pin you down, but it was like you were pushing him back with your eyes. What was it?' I asked urgently, thinking back to the scene. It was more than just pushing Samuel back. I glanced at her peculiar pupils again. What else could she do?

'To be honest, I'm not sure what I did to him. I just focused all my energy into hurting him, and that's what happened,' Mary Jane said. 'Thank goodness you found me. I'd be dead otherwise. Why were you down at the docks, anyway?'

'I was following Samuel, hoping he would lead me to where he's keeping my brother, Damon. Then I realised he'd captured you. Do you know why?'

'I think he was trailing me. This time, he got me,' she said, knitting her eyebrows together. 'I've seen him a few times around the East End, near the lodging house where I work as a maid. I only noticed him because he's not the usual type we see in those parts. And then when everyone was talking about how the Ripper may have been a count or something . . . well, I paid attention. You can't be too careful these days.'

'Did you know the girls who were killed?'

Mary Jane shook her head. 'No, I didn't. I just keep my head down and do my work.'

'So why did Samuel attack you?' Cora asked.

'How would I know?' Mary Jane replied in exasperation. 'It wasn't on my mind to ask him why when he was grabbing me right off the street.'

'It's fine, Mary Jane,' I interjected. 'Just tell us what happened.'

'I'd got off work early and was about to meet my friends for a pint,' she explained. 'But as I walked by an alleyway, he came out of nowhere and snatched me up. I tried screaming and kicking, but we were going too fast for anyone to notice. At first, I thought I was being taken by Jack the Ripper. But he isn't, is he? Because why would a vampire kill like that?'

'You just asked the million-pound question,' Cora said.

Before I could explain further a rat came out of its hiding spot. I reached for a stone, ready to attack. But Mary Jane held up a hand.

'I've got it,' she said, placing her fingers on the floor. 'Shh! Come here, love,' she cooed at the animal. The rat halted and cocked its head at her. 'Right here,' she urged. Quickly, the rat ran onto her palm and stood on its hind legs. She raised her eyebrows at us and smiled crookedly. 'See, they're not so bad.'

'How did you learn to do that?' I asked.

She shrugged. 'I didn't learn. I was born like this.'

'And your parents . . . ?'

'Are dead,' she said flatly.

'I'm sorry,' Cora and I said in unison.

A flicker of a smile crossed Mary Jane's face. 'Or they might as well be. They might be alive somewhere, but I don't rightly know. I don't know anything about my parents. I only know that I've always had a sense about people, and animals, and can sometimes have them do what I want.'

'Do you think you can help us?' I asked eagerly. My stomach rumbled, and I had to turn away to avoid automatically reaching out and killing the rodent cupped in Mary Jane's hands.

'I could try. I've never really used my spells on vampires before,' she said uncertainly. 'I've never used them for anything important. Just for little things. To make the rent collector go away, or to get a rat to do tricks like this. But I don't know if I'm strong enough to defeat a vampire. Unless . . . I have friends who could help,' she finished, letting the rat free. It squeaked, then skittered away into the shadows. 'Only I'm not sure they'll like you. We keep to ourselves, mainly. But I'll tell them you saved me. I can't say whether that'll sway them, seeing as you kill our kind, but I can take you to them.'

'That would be very kind,' I said. 'Are your friends like you?'

'You mean, are they witches?' Mary Jane asked matter-of-factly. 'Well, I suppose so. Although I don't know what makes a witch a witch. But I do know we all have magical powers,' she said, giving me a lopsided smile. I smiled back encouragingly.

'How many?' Cora breathed.

'Not many. There's just five of us. Me, Billy, Gus and Vivian. And Jemima of course, but she's—'

'She's what?' I asked.

'She's the one who might not like you,' Mary Jane said. 'She doesn't trust others. But when I tell her that you saved my life, she might reconsider.'

'But the rest of them?' I asked.

A fond smile crossed her face. 'They're lovely. They're my family, really. I never had a proper one. When I was twelve, I thought I'd be adopted. I used to dream about what it'd be like to have a mother, a home and a bed with a feather mattress . . .' She shook her head and set her mouth in a firm line. 'That didn't come true. But I got something better. I got people who'd never let me down.'

I nodded. I had so many questions and scarcely knew where to begin. A memory from years before flashed through my mind. I'd been sitting on a rock in the middle of the forest on the edge of Mystic Falls, listening to Katherine explain how she'd turned others into vampires like her. But witches were different. They didn't *become* witches – they were born witches. The craft was in their blood.

'How did you find the others?' Cora asked softly. Her knees were pulled close to her chest, and she looked like a child being told a bedtime story.

'Well, once you know what you're looking for, you start

to notice things,' Mary Jane explained. 'Jemima and I found each other first. We were in the same orphanage together, and as soon as she came in, I realised she was special. She could *fix* things. Her chores would magically get done while she was in bed sleeping. Or she'd accidentally spill ink on a book, and seconds later it would look good as new. I finally got the courage to ask her about it, and then we started working on spells together.'

Hope flickered in me. It sounded like Mary Jane and Jemima were both very powerful. If so, then maybe we really did have a chance at defeating Samuel. Although he was strong, magic overrode all other Powers. We had to do anything we could to get Jemima to agree to help us.

'What about the others?' Cora asked.

Mary Jane wrinkled her forehead. 'Well, I saw Vivian making a concoction with some leftover whisky at a tavern where she was a scullery maid. Gus was a paperboy who Jemima saw talking to sparrows in his spare time. And we found Billy putting a spell on a roll he was eating outside a bakery. Before he took the last bite, he conjured up four more fresh ones.' She smiled.

'It will be a pleasure to meet them,' I said. A witch, a human and a vampire, teaming up to fight evil. It sounded like the premise of a penny-paper serial. But thanks to the monster who was plotting our deaths, this was our real lives.

CHAPTER 4

The next day, Cora and I followed Mary Jane to the home she shared with the orphans. The foggy, grey morning matched my mood. What if Mary Jane's friends wouldn't help? Or what if it was too late to save Damon? Out of the tunnel, I could see the dark circles under Mary Jane's eyes, the frayed hem of her faded brown dress. She looked every inch the orphan she was. No matter how hard I tried to push it out of my mind, I kept wondering: if she was so powerful, why wasn't she able to rise in society? Why were she and her witch friends living in such a slum? Damon would have wanted to know. But I didn't. Because why did it matter? The point was, she was all we had.

'Here we are. Home sweet home,' Mary Jane said brightly as she turned a tight corner into a tiny alley. The buildings on either side of the street were dilapidated, with boarded-up windows and, in some cases, huge holes in their outer walls.

She pushed her shoulder against a door and let Cora and me step inside.

I blinked in the dark foyer of the hovel that Mary Jane called home, taking in the uneven ceiling, the sloped floor missing half its boards and the endless strands of cobwebs glimmering in the darkness.

'Shh.' Mary Jane put a cautionary finger to her lips as she crept up the staircase – if it could be called that. The banister had been ripped from the wall and several steps had rotted away. The ones that remained were off-kilter, and it seemed a miracle – or magic – that the entire house hadn't collapsed.

At the top of the stairs, Mary Jane opened a flimsy door. 'I'm home!' she announced grandly.

I blinked. In the centre of room was a fire, ringed and contained by concrete slabs most likely stolen from the street. A skylight was directly above it. The glass must have fallen out long ago, leaving only a gaping hole that offered a view of the cloudy sky. Around the fire sat two boys and one girl, all no older than eighteen. One of the boys, the youngest, looked like he was only twelve. The room smelled of mildew and damp. I coughed.

'Mary Jane!' The youngest boy sprang up and wrapped

his bony arms around Mary Jane's waist. She smiled fondly and ruffled his blond hair. 'You're home! I thought the Ripper got you!'

'Don't be upset, Gus. I'm home now. But it's all thanks to Stefan here. If it wasn't for him, I would have been hacked to pieces,' she explained.

'By the R-r-ripper?' Gus asked, stuttering in fear.

'Worse than that,' she said. 'Stefan and Cora, this is Gus, Vivian and Billy. My family. Jemima must be in another room,' she added, making a short introduction to the group sitting round the fire. I wondered whether she would tell them I was a vampire. I wondered if they, too, knew just by looking at me.

'What's worse than Jack the Ripper?' the girl, who must have been Vivian, asked in disbelief. Her lilting voice held an Irish accent similar to Cora's. Cora perked up, but didn't speak.

'A vampire,' Mary Jane said simply. At the word, the orphans all turned to stare at me. Gus's jaw dropped, and I wondered if, like Mary Jane, they immediately knew my true nature.

'While I was on my way to meet up with you lot last night, I got taken from the streets and brought down to the docks,' Mary Jane explained. 'Luckily, Stefan here saved me before my attacker could do any real damage.'

'Yes, but why was Stefan there in the first place?' the older boy asked, rising to his feet and glaring at me. 'He's a vampire too, you know.'

I stepped forward, turning my palms to the air as if to show I had nothing to hide. 'I am a vampire, it's true. But *that* vampire, Samuel, kidnapped my brother. He's evil, and he'll stop at nothing to get what he wants. And what he wants includes Mary Jane. I was only able to wound him, and he'll be back. Soon.' My gaze flicked between the witches. I knew I somehow had to convince them that Samuel was a worthy enemy – one we needed to work together to defeat.

'So why are you *here*?' Gus asked. It was clear from the tone of his voice that his terror had turned into mistrust. He was wearing spectacles, and the flames reflected in them gave his moon-shaped, pimpled face a vaguely sinister sheen.

'Because we need witches on our side to fight Samuel,' I said simply.

'What if we say no?' the older boy asked, crossing his arms and stepping towards me as if he were challenging me to a fight.

'Billy!' Mary Jane said sharply, putting her hands on her hips and glaring at him. Then she turned to me. 'Sorry. As I'm sure you know, we don't trust vampires as a rule. But you're different than most. We just have to adjust.'

'If you saved Mary Jane, then I trust you,' Vivian said shyly. She looked about fifteen years old and had long curly brown hair that fanned over her thin shoulders. The irises of her eyes were so dark her pupils seemed to disappear into them.

'Vivian helps with our spells,' Mary Jane said by way of introduction. 'She reads all the spell books, then she works out how to say it.'

The girl nodded proudly, a flicker of a smile crossing her face. 'I do,' she affirmed. 'Mostly I'm successful, but I'll admit there are still some improvements I could make.'

'She set the last place we lived on fire,' Gus piped up.

'I did not! It was just a little hole in the floor. Gus, stop being dramatic.'

'Well, whatever spells you can do would be a huge help,' I interrupted before the conversation turned into a verbal sparring match. 'We know where Samuel lives. We know he's the culprit behind the Jack the Ripper killings. And we know that something Mary Jane did staved him off. Now all we have to do is figure out how we can strengthen that spell and find a way to catch him off guard.'

'What did you do?' Gus asked Mary Jane suspiciously. I noticed he was wearing layers of newspapers tied to his feet instead of shoes and I wondered how badly off the orphans were. Couldn't they use magic to procure clothes, or did some code of honesty prevent that?

'Well, that's just the thing, Gus. I don't know. He attacked me and threw me to the ground, and I kept thinking of the magnets Vivian had shown us a while back,' Mary Jane explained as she sat and warmed her hands by the fire. I noticed Cora hugging her body tightly. I heard the wind whistling around the room and could see Mary Jane's breath as she spoke. I nudged Cora, urging her to stand nearer to the fire, but she stayed at my side.

Vivian leaned excitedly towards Mary Jane. 'So the repel spell worked?'

'Well, sort of,' Mary Jane said. 'I couldn't hold it for too long. Samuel broke through and was about to kill me, but then Stefan stepped in.'

'All right,' Gus said, turning his attention to me. 'So, let's say we do come up with a few spells to defeat Samuel and help you save your brother. What's in it for us? Why should we risk our lives for you?'

'I can get you out of here,' I said confidently. 'Into a far better home.'

'Can you, vampire?' The door slammed shut as a girl entered the room. She strode towards me and pressed her index finger into my chest. Her face was all angles, reminding me of a bird, and her dishwater-blonde hair was lifeless and strawlike. She wasn't pretty, except for her large grey eyes, which darted back and forth as if she were a wolf tracking its prey. It was clear that Jemima acted as the ringleader of this particular group, simultaneously serving as both mother and disciplinarian. I knew she was trying to protect the house, but I still didn't appreciate her distrustful gaze.

Beneath her touch, my skin began to burn. I shifted uncomfortably. What was she doing?

'I'm Stefan, and this is my friend Cora. We're friends of Mary Jane's. I saved her life last night.'

'So I heard. The house isn't exactly big. I know who you are. And how exactly do you plan to get us out of here? Will you lie? Compel? Kill a family, then steal their home?'

'Jemima, stop it,' Mary Jane said sharply. 'We owe him something.'

'I don't owe him anything,' Jemima said, keeping her steady gaze on me. 'Mary Jane, you almost got killed. I know he saved you, but how do you know he has your best interests at heart? You know vampires don't have beating hearts, let alone souls. That's why—' She stopped short. 'That's why I need to ask him a few questions. Get him to reveal his intentions,' she said cryptically.

'Go ahead, I have no secrets,' I said. *The truth shall set you free.* It had been one of my father's favourite quotations and his motivation for naming our Virginia estate Veritas –

Latin for 'truth'. I hoped the wisdom applied equally to vampires and humans.

'How many people have you killed?' Jemima asked, her voice dropping to a whisper.

I glanced round the room, knowing nobody would like my answers. Even Cora was gazing at me quizzically, a hardened expression in her eyes. In the semi-darkness, surrounded by six pairs of glittering eyes, I felt like the witches could peer into my mind and know what I was thinking even before I said it. I had to tell the truth. But I wasn't even sure if I knew it myself.

I racked my brain, pulling memories from Mystic Falls and New Orleans as if turning back the pages of a book. I knew every painful detail of my first kill – my father. I remembered the sweet, smoky blood of Clementine Haverford, the fresh, lilac-scented blood of my victim on the train to New Orleans, as well as all the faceless humans who just happened to be in the wrong place at the wrong time . . .

'Can't even remember, can you?' Jemima asked in disgust. 'See, their destruction has no boundaries.'

'I have killed, it's true. More than I wish I had. But I haven't in a long time, and I don't feed on humans,' I said, choosing my words carefully.

Jemima's flinty grey eyes softened slightly, 'That, at least, is the truth.'

'It's all I have,' I said. 'I can't change the past. But I want to change the future. And I don't want Samuel to kill my brother.'

'So is that how you see it?' Jemima asked, turning to the witches as if she were a barrister speaking to a jury. 'Because you saved Mary Jane's life, we owe it to you to save your brother's life?'

'If that's how you want to see it, yes.'

I expected Jemima to argue. But instead, she merely laughed, a sharp snort, punctuating the tense silence that had fallen in the room.

'You're smart, vampire. You know better than to lie your way into my good graces. I think we might be able to work something out. Besides, I don't like vampires, so I'm all for getting rid of one who's been causing trouble.'

'Thank you,' I said gratefully.

Jemima held up her hand. 'Don't thank me till I've done something. Of course, the fact that you don't feed on human blood comes with complications, doesn't it? Vivian, we're going to need some eleuthro. Actually, better find enough for the lot of us,' she said. Instantly, Vivian scrambled to her feet and raced down the stairs. Jemima leaned towards me. I flinched, sure she was about to touch me and set off the same burning sensation she had a few minutes ago. But she didn't. Instead, she yanked a single hair from my head.

'What's eleuthro?' I asked, my tongue tripping over the unfamiliar word.

'A potion,' Jemima said briefly. 'But don't you worry about that. First things first, let's find where Samuel is keeping your brother.' She dropped the strand of hair into the fire. 'What's his name?'

'Damon. Damon Salvatore,' I said, picturing the classic half-smirk my brother wore when he introduced himself to women. But my thoughts were interrupted by Jemima's chant.

> Two blood brothers, separated by land or sea
> With this lock bring him to thee.
> Show us Damon, not for game, or sport, or play
> But so from evil we can lift him away.

'Now, let's hope it works,' she muttered as she stepped back, allowing Billy to stoke the fire. He circled the blaze in an anticlockwise motion, causing the room to fill with smoke. The greyish-white billows began to fan out. I blinked as a purple cloud formed directly above the flames. In its centre was a hazy image of Damon. He was tied to a column, his eyes drooping and his body trembling. He was clearly starving and racked with pain. Ropes bound him to scaffolding, and I knew from the enormous welts apparent in the vision that they must have been soaked with vervain.

I squinted, trying to pick out some sort of clue in the background. In the distance, far beyond Damon's shoulder, was a hulking edifice. But was that still part of the vision, or was it a trick of the light? I felt a painful pounding in my temple.

'It looks like Tower Bridge,' I murmured, walking closer and closer to the image. I could make out the foundation and the deck, with Damon's body affixed to one of the girders. All of a sudden, I heard a loud sizzle. The image disappeared and I realised Jemima had poured a large bucket of water onto the fire. Sparks jumped around me.

'Why did you do that?' I'd only begun to pick apart the vision for clues. Yes, it was Tower Bridge, but *why*? Where was Samuel? How long had Damon been there? And how long would he survive?

'Saving you from yourself, vampire,' Jemima said, grimacing. 'You were so close to the fire you were about to fall in. And then where would we be?'

I took a few steps back, seating myself in a chair in the far corner of the room, trying to figure out how I could use what I had seen in the fire to rescue Damon.

The door opened, and Vivian entered the room holding a tarnished silver pitcher. 'I made the potion. I had plenty of the herb, but I had to guess the amounts of mugwort and dragonroot,' she fretted.

'It doesn't matter,' Jemima said, but I saw her gaze nervously cut to Mary Jane. So far, all their spells seemed to have worked. But what happened when one didn't?

Vivian took a small sip, wiped her Cupid's-bow mouth with the back of her hand and passed the pitcher to Mary Jane, who followed suit.

'Makes you stronger,' Mary Jane explained as she passed the pitcher to me.

'Really?' I asked, looking dubiously at the liquid sloshing inside the container. The greenish colour reminded me of sludge culled from the bottom of a pond. I sniffed it. It smelled like burning leaves.

'You have nothing to lose, vampire,' Jemima said sharply.

'True.' I took a large drink, as if to prove to her I wasn't afraid of the potion – or her. The liquid bubbled down my throat. It tasted fetid and vile, as if it were made of the refuse filling the streets.

'I'll need some, too,' Cora said, plucking the pitcher from my hands and taking several deep gulps as though she were one of the tavern girls holding her own in a pint-drinking competition with dock labourers.

'Good girl,' Jemima said, sounding impressed. The boys drank from the pitcher in turn. 'And now that we've all drunk up, it's time to go. Who knows how long he'll be at the bridge.'

I felt stronger, and my throbbing headache had disappeared. The eleuthro was better than blood. It took the edge off my nerves and made me feel like I could take on anyone – or anything. I experimentally squeezed the arm of a nearby chair, thrilled to see the wood snap like a twig between my fingers.

'Confident the potion works, vampire?' Jemima asked, her hands on her hips.

'Yes,' I said testily. 'And I'm sorry I broke the chair, but this makes a good stake. We need more weapons like this, just in case,' I said. It was true. The slim chair arm tapered into a sharp point that would easily pierce through skin. I hastily turned to address all the witches. 'Damon will most likely be tied up with vervain-soaked ropes. Vervain's poisonous to me, so I can't untie him. Could one of you set him free? The herb won't hurt you.'

'I will,' Billy volunteered, heading to the remains of the chair to create more makeshift stakes.

'Thank you,' I said. 'Jemima, are there any spells you can perform that could help?'

'Are there *any* spells I can perform?' Jemima repeated sarcastically. I sucked in my breath, annoyed at the literal way she took my words but knowing far better than to say anything.

'What spell do you think would be best?' I asked patiently.

'Leave that to me, vampire,' Jemima said. 'I'm not sharing all my secrets with you. I know you're honest, but I still can't trust you. And I won't know what spell to perform until I see Samuel for myself.'

'What can I do?' Gus asked, stepping up to me.

I appraised the skinny boy, then glanced at Jemima. She nodded at me, as if giving me permission to speak. 'Why don't you watch out for Cora,' I decided.

'I don't need looking out for,' Cora retorted.

'I know. But if Samuel and Violet are there, then—'

'Then I want to fight them,' Cora said, cutting me off.

'And aren't you forgetting something, vampire?' Jemima smirked.

'What?' I asked. We had stakes, we had spells . . .

'How do you plan to carry this off at Tower Bridge? There are always people around. You really need a blocking spell, so no one walks in on us.'

'Yes!' I exclaimed. Despite Jemima's sarcasm, her suggestion proved she was listening and ready to help.

'Vampires just don't think about details,' she muttered. 'Gus and Mary Jane, can you do a simple circle spell when we get to the bridge? We don't want any mortals getting caught in the ruckus.'

'Thank you,' I said meaningfully, locking eyes with Jemima.

She didn't respond, but the corners of her mouth twisted into a small smile.

And with all the witches on board, we streamed towards the door, ready to free my brother.

'Damon, I'm coming,' I whispered under my breath. But the only response was the ominous sound of rain pelting the roof.

CHAPTER 5

Together, stakes concealed under our clothing, our motley group traipsed through the back alleys of London's East End. What had been a cloudy day had turned into a bitterly cold and rainy evening. Cora shivered beside me.

As we walked past a public house where a few men hunched over their pints of ale, Mary Jane hurried to catch up with me. I forced myself to take slow, measured steps, but it was hard to walk at human speed with the eleuthro surging through my veins. All my senses were heightened, and I breathed in the stench of rotting garbage in the gutter. As pungent as the scent was, it was a poor distraction from the sound of blood pumping round me. While it may have taken the edge off my nerves, the eleuthro hadn't assuaged my craving. If anything, it had intensified it.

'The first rule we have when performing magic is not to draw any attention to ourselves,' Mary Jane said, pulling me back to the conversation. I hadn't been paying attention. I was so distracted by the thought of blood that I could almost taste it on my tongue. I knew it was simply because we were in the East End, which was packed with residents. The more humans, the greater concentration of blood. That was one of the many reasons I'd preferred my life in a quaint village where neighbours were few and far between. It was easier to ignore the call of blood.

'I was saying, we try to blend in to our surroundings,' Mary Jane said patiently, when she saw I wasn't exactly focused. 'The second rule is, no magic in public, unless we're threatened by death. Of course, we'll use magic to free your brother, but we must maintain a low profile. If any one of us is exposed, we're immediately kicked out of the house. It's Jemima's rule, and she means it. The third rule is no talking about magic, for the same reason as not performing it.'

'Can all of you do the same magic?' Cora asked.

'Not quite.' Mary Jane wrinkled her forehead in concentration. 'Some are good at spells, others more at finding herbs, and I'm good with animals. I suppose we all work better when we're together. We protect one another. Anyway, as soon as Jemima and I realised we were different, we ran away from the orphanage and didn't look back. Once we all found one another, we didn't need to wait around for someone to adopt us. Adoptions never seemed to happen.

People would always come in and say we were precious, or say we were special, but then they never came back to bring us home,' Mary Jane said sadly. 'That's why it was better for us to form our own family.'

'Shh!' Jemima hissed, whirling round. She took the hood of my cloak and pulled it over my head. 'Try to be inconspicuous, please.'

'Sorry,' I muttered.

'Rule number four. We stick together. Once we get there, there's no running off, and there's no leaving anyone behind, even if it's dangerous. Are we clear?' I nodded.

We walked onto the pier. The Thames was crowded with cargo ships ready to make their early morning deliveries at ports dotting the country, while smaller passenger ships wove around them.

'We'll go by river,' Jemima decided, nodding to a small skiff floating in the water. The name *Goodspeed* was written on its side. I decided to take that as a good sign. 'A boat gives us an automatic escape route. Climb on,' she said grandly as we all jumped over the edge and into our stolen boat.

As Billy pushed the *Goodspeed* away from the dock, I looked towards the inky horizon. The skiff was moving of its own volition, cutting a V-shaped path through the water.

I could sense Jemima's eyes on the back of my neck. I turned round. Sure enough, she was staring at me, an inscrutable expression on her face.

'What?' I asked irritably. I had a sense she knew more than she was letting on.

'Just trying to figure out how hungry you are, vampire.'

'I fed on a squirrel today. I'm not thinking of drinking human blood, if that's what you're wondering.'

'Not that kind of hunger,' Jemima said cryptically. She nodded towards something behind me and I whirled round, seeing the imposing Tower Bridge now only a hundred feet in front of us. It stood several storeys off the ground, and was surrounded by wooden scaffolding. The deck of the bridge came to an abrupt end a quarter of the way across the river; across the Thames, a similar set-up was in place. A gap of forty feet separating the two structures. I was surprised that no watchmen were guarding the area. Instead, all was silent, except for the sound of ragged breathing. It was Damon. It had to be.

'Pull over to the dock!' I called. Immediately, without anyone steering, the skiff turned to the nearest pier. I jumped onto the dock before the boat stopped. Clutching my stake to my side, I ran towards the bridge. The closer I got, the more I was sure I was being watched.

I glanced up and gasped.

Instead of seeing Damon, I saw Samuel clinging like a spider to the underside of the bridge. He jumped down on top of me, throwing me off balance. I landed on my back with a thud.

'And so we meet again,' Samuel said, standing over me, his face a blank mask that betrayed no emotion. Our eyes locked, and for a fraction of a second it was as if time stood still. Then Violet emerged from behind a pillar, smiling maniacally, her white fangs glittering. She was a completely different creature than the frightened girl I'd rescued a month earlier. In a white fur coat with her red curls piled on top of her head and her lips painted a deep crimson, she looked like a painting come to life. She wasn't the innocent Irish barmaid I'd met at the Ten Bells Tavern. She wasn't the giddy show-off who'd blushed and twirled when I'd bought her a new dress at Harrods. And she certainly wasn't the human girl who'd looked at me with tears in her eyes as she transitioned into a vampire, begging me to kill her rather than allow her to live a life of destruction. That Violet was dead. The fiend in front of me was all vampire.

Samuel shifted, and I used the momentary movement to spring to my feet and lunge, surprised at how fast the eleuthro had made me. Grabbing his shoulders, I wrestled him to the ground. He twisted free and I hurled myself at him again, smiling when his head smacked against the concrete bridge with a satisfying crack.

'Stefan!'

I whipped my head round at the sound of my name. Damon was fixed to the scaffolding by vervain-soaked ropes as if he were a sacrificial figure primed for an ancient ritual. He exhaled in wet gasps, and blood-tinged foam frothed at the corners of his mouth. The veins around his temples were bulging and were an unnatural bright-blue colour. He looked minutes away from death.

'Help him!' I called to the witches. I couldn't save him right now, not with Samuel here and Damon covered in vervain. Billy raced past me with a knife held aloft, ready to cut Damon loose from the ropes that bound him.

I gripped my stake and reared back, about to strike, when suddenly I was hit from behind. Violet must have caught up with us. I landed on my chest, my body only an inch away from falling on the stake. I struggled to a sitting position, but Violet threw herself on top of me, pinning my shoulders to the ground as she groped for the stake.

I heard a splash. Samuel had thrown Vivian and Gus into the cold water. They were sputtering while Jemima and Mary Jane were fighting Samuel off with the repel spell. It was almost working. But not well enough.

I knew Violet was out for blood, and if she couldn't get mine, she'd think nothing of taking her sister's. With a surge of effort, I wriggled out of her hold and managed to pin her hands to the ground above her shoulders. 'Samuel will die tonight. I'll make sure of it. But I'm giving you one last chance,' I said, searching for any trace of humanity in her bloodshot eyes. But all Violet did was laugh in response.

Just then, I saw Cora racing towards us, far faster than a normal human could move. 'Cora, get away!' I shouted. Violet was strong and I doubted that Cora would come close to matching her, even aided by eleuthro.

'No. Violet, listen to me,' she said, throwing her arms around her waist. 'I'm your sister. I know you. And I know you have a chance for redemption. Please, stop what you're doing and take it.' Cora's voice dropped to a whisper. 'Or else I'll kill you myself.' At this, Violet stopped writhing and turned to face her sister.

'Not if I kill you first.' She growled as she lunged towards Cora, her fangs dangerously close to her sister's throat. Her eyes were large and red, and in that moment she was a vampire intent only on her kill – even though her prey was her own flesh and blood. I clutched the wooden stake in one hand as I grabbed her from behind and threw her on her back.

I was about to bring the weapon down when another stake sliced through the air and plunged into the rich fur of Violet's coat. She unleashed an agonised shriek before falling limp. Her skin quickly turned ashen and veiny, her mouth frozen as if gasping for air. She was dead.

Cora sat back, a hand to her lips in shock. She was staring, unblinking, at the body of her sister. The sister she had just killed.

Not able to take even a moment to grieve Violet's tragic, if necessary, death, I turned to aid Mary Jane and Jemima in fighting off Samuel. This fight wasn't over.

But Samuel was no longer standing with the witches. Instead, he was high above, teetering on the edge of the bridge. Before I could begin to scramble up the scaffolding, he dived into the water, as gracefully as a gull swooping down to catch a fish. A splash, and Samuel was in the middle of the Thames, arms stroking toward the opposite bank.

I blinked in disbelief. The repel spell Mary Jane and Jemima had used was working – Samuel had run away. Still, I didn't feel victorious that he'd retreated from the fight. Samuel must have realised he was outnumbered and didn't stand a chance against us. But although we may have won this battle, Samuel was preparing for war. *At least we saved Damon*, I thought as I hurried over to where Jemima was inspecting his injuries.

'Brother.' Damon nodded. Angry burn marks circling his wrists oozed blood; his skin was pockmarked with burns, scrapes, cuts and dirt; his lips were cracked; and one of his eyes was swollen shut. He looked in worse shape than he had when he'd been beaten, starved and bitten by alligators at Gallagher's Circus in New Orleans. He needed blood – a lot of it.

My heart thudded in my chest as our eyes met. I'd saved his life. So why did I have nothing to say?

'Go feed,' I said roughly. Seeing him so weak shook me. I knew that if we'd waited only an hour longer, chances are he'd have been dead. And that was a possibility I wouldn't let myself think about. 'You'll find some victims further down the pier.'

But Damon didn't move. I was the one who looked away, turning my attention to Cora, kneeling next to the body of her sister. She slowly took Violet's hands and rested them in a praying position on her still chest. Then she turned to me, her face slicked with tears.

'She's really dead. I killed her,' she said quietly.

'You didn't kill her. *Samuel* killed her. What you killed was the monster in Violet's body,' I said. But it wasn't that simple. I knew better than anyone that your soul didn't simply disappear when you became a vampire. Violet *had* been in there, somewhere, but most likely her spirit had been beaten badly as a result of committing far too many murders. I knew she would never have been the same.

'No, Stefan.' Cora looked up and shook her head sadly. 'I killed her. And now there's no hope she'll ever become a vampire like you. One who *cares* about others. And that's all my fault. I'll never forgive myself.'

'Don't do that,' Damon rasped. Cora turned to him questioningly. 'Say goodbye to Violet, then let her go. She wouldn't want you to hold on. Letting go is the only thing you can do,' he said thickly.

He picked up the lifeless body and brought it to the edge of the river. On the bank, the witches were standing with their backs towards us, giving us privacy by ensuring the circle spell remained in place.

Cora nodded and brought her lips to Violet's forehead. 'Goodbye,' she murmured.

Then Damon threw the body into the river. It rose once to the surface before sinking into the murky water. As soon as it did, Cora broke off into a torrent of sobs. I pulled her to me, smoothing her hair.

Your first death changes you.

It was something Damon had told me when I'd mourned my fiancée, Rosalyn. At that point, he had already seen countless deaths on the battlefield. But so, I realised, had Cora. She'd been pulled into our war as an innocent bystander, and already she'd witnessed the murders of two friends and the torture and death of Samuel's brother. But Violet was different. Violet was her sister, and Cora had been the one to kill her.

She continued to sob into my chest. 'Damon needs your help,' I said finally, pulling back.

'I know.' She turned away from Violet's watery grave and followed me towards my brother. Cora was strong – I only wished we hadn't learned that the hard way.

CHAPTER 6

The woman thrown into the rushing river with a stake protruding from her chest was a monster who would have killed her own sister if given half a chance. She was bloodthirsty, angry and savage; a beast in the guise of a beautiful girl.

Twenty years ago, my father created his own history for Damon and me, one in which we were glorious, fallen heroes. He'd wanted Jonathan Gilbert to write in the town ledger that Damon and I had died fighting in a skirmish against Union soldiers. He had wanted his sons to be good, upstanding men. Not protectors of monsters, which was how my father saw my brother's and my desperate attempts to save Katherine, the woman we loved.

I knew how he felt. Because more than anything I wished Violet had died as the epitome of evil incarnate. But I knew I had to think of the true Violet. Yes, she was a bloodthirsty monster, but she'd also been the young, idealistic girl who had set sail across the Irish Sea with her sister in search of fame, fortune and romance.

The thought led me again to Katherine. She was the truth at the centre of an infinitely complicated riddle. Because of her, I no longer knew good from evil. After all, there was an undeniable monstrous, murderous streak within me. I only hoped I could draw on it to bring down Samuel and live a legacy of honour and victory.

The next morning, I woke up and found myself staring at a vaulted, rotting ceiling high above me. I was back in the witches' slum, and although Damon was free, Samuel had escaped into the Thames. A few feet away, I could see that Billy, Vivian and Jemima were sitting around the open fire.

'They need to leave,' a voice near the fire murmured. The witches clearly weren't aware I was awake. I knew the voice belonged to Gus. He must still be wrapped in blankets and shivering in front of the fire after his fall in the river.

'They have nowhere to go,' Mary Jane's voice said firmly.

'But Gus and Vivian were almost killed last night. We spent long enough forming this family. I won't just watch it be destroyed.' Jemima didn't bother keeping her voice down, and the message was clear: we weren't wanted and she wanted us to know it.

I struggled to sit up, surprised to see Cora sitting next to the fire, flanked by Jemima and Mary Jane.

'Stefan saved Mary Jane's life. He deserves your help,' Cora piped up.

'We settled that debt. We helped him get his brother back – and we're close to pneumonia for our efforts. At the end of the day, Stefan is a vampire. Look where helping him got you,' Jemima said to Cora, not unkindly. 'You took a chance on him, and he forced you into battle with your sister.'

'*He* didn't *force* anything. And I wouldn't have killed Violet if she'd truly been herself. But my sister died weeks ago – that was a demon who died back there,' Cora countered.

'Whatever gets you through the day,' Jemima said dismissively.

I staggered to my feet. 'There's no need for us to stay. We'll go. Thanks for all your help,' I said. In truth, I was eager to get back to the tunnel. It may not have had creature comforts, but I felt it was far safer than a room full of witches.

Just then, Damon unleashed a guttural groan from the corner of the room. Sweat poured from his hairline and Cora rushed to tend to him. 'He's burning up. He should be healed by now. I'm going to give him more blood.' Cora slicked back the hair from his forehead. Despite my suggestion at the bridge, he'd never properly fed. Even when Cora had cut her skin and held it up to his mouth, he'd only taken a few tentative sips. Ever since we'd saved him, Damon had been quiet. And a quiet Damon always made me uneasy.

I didn't stop her as she pushed up her sleeve and unwrapped a muslin cloth from her wrist, uncovering the wound she'd made yesterday. She scratched a scab, and a small trickle of blood ran onto her skin. I quickly turned away. I wondered if she'd hidden the unhealed wound from me on purpose, so I wouldn't be tempted. My heart twisted at the thought.

'Damon,' she said, shaking his shoulders slightly. 'Wake up.'

'Heart,' he murmured, thrashing. 'He needs a heart.' I leaned down and tried to listen to the words. What did Damon mean? *Who* needed a heart?

'Shh, wake up,' Cora murmured, holding her wrist to his mouth. He began to drink, but his eyes were still squeezed shut. Cora winced as his fangs grazed her skin, and I was aware of the witches watching us as though we were performing a macabre play. They shifted uncomfortably. Jemima huffed, and I knew she didn't want blood-drinking to take place under her roof.

Damon paused mid-drink and a grimace crossed his

face. Then, he curled his upper lip, as though readying for an attack.

'Cora!' I hissed.

'That's enough,' Cora said firmly, extricating her wrist from Damon's fangs.

He sat up and blinked, pushing the blankets away.

'Where am I?' he sputtered.

'You're somewhere safer than hanging from Tower Bridge, that's for sure,' I said. Damon lifted his gaze to meet mine and nodded imperceptibly. His normally blue eyes appeared muddy, as if they had witnessed a host of unspeakable horrors. My mind drifted to the latest theory the papers had printed regarding the Jack the Ripper murders: some doctors believed people's eyes recorded the last image they saw before they died. Physicians from London University Hospital postulated that all the Metropolitan Police had to do to catch Jack the Ripper was to photograph the faces of his victims, examine the negatives, and identify any hazy figure reflected in their eyes. So far, they hadn't had any luck with the theory, but looking at the despair in Damon's eyes now, I could understand where the idea came from.

'Are you all right?' Mary Jane asked with concern.

'I will be,' he said. His voice sounded rough and scratchy, as if he hadn't used it in a long time. He spotted the crimson trickle of blood on Cora's skin and reflexively bared his fangs. Not meeting his gaze, she carefully retied the muslin, which immediately bloomed with a rosette of fresh blood. I glanced away, but not before a terrible, unbidden thought once again crossed my mind: *why not drink human blood?*

'I have a spell that might help,' Vivian said shyly. 'It's just some lilac water and words,' she added, pulling a few sprigs of purple flowers from the pocket of her dress. She took a few of the leaves and dropped them in the pitcher that had held the eleuthro the night before. She swirled the mixture, muttering under her breath, then passed the concoction to Damon.

'You want me to drink your flower water?' he asked sceptically. I was relieved to hear a trace of his old, caustic self in his voice.

'I do,' Vivian said, rocking back on her heels. Her voice was soft but steady.

Damon shut his eyes and gingerly took a sip. Damon, the man who could easily down a few stiff whiskies, was nervous about drinking a potion.

'Finish it off,' Vivian urged.

He choked down a few more sips. Already, he looked better. The colour had returned to his cheeks and his eyes had lost their haunted look. He was definitely well enough to make the journey back through London.

'I never thought I'd have to depend on witches to save

me,' he said. 'But I suppose we live in strange times.' He turned to Mary Jane. 'Let's just hope you continue to stay safe from Samuel.'

My ears pricked up. 'What do you mean?' I asked urgently.

'He wants her,' Damon said. He jerked his elbow towards Mary Jane. 'That's why he's been ripping humans apart. He's hoping one of his victims might be a witch.'

'What? Why me?' Mary Jane asked, her voice rising in panic. 'I didn't do anything to him.'

'It's not what you did, it's who you *are*,' Damon said cryptically. 'Apparently, you're a purebred witch. And your heart is of great value to them.'

'A purebred witch?' I repeated dumbly. 'What does that mean?'

'It's a witch descended from the very first coven – the Original coven. Samuel and Seaver researched the bloodlines of purebred witches and discovered the last known descendant had been living in an East End orphanage. They believe *you*, Mary Jane, are the one they've been looking for.'

'It sounds like a load of nonsense, vampire,' Jemima said. 'And I won't have you saying things like that under my roof. Spreading lies and frightening everyone to death.'

'You don't have to believe me.' Damon shrugged. 'All I know is what I heard them say.'

Mary Jane's face turned white. 'But I don't know who my family is. So how could Samuel know?'

'Vampires are craftier than you'd think,' Cora said. I glanced sharply at her. 'And Samuel can be relentless when he wants something.'

'You're right.' Jemima nodded briefly. 'If there's a vampire after our Mary Jane, we need to get out of here as soon as possible. I'm sure he knows where we live. Mary Jane, you need to hide. I'll come with you.' She turned to me expectantly.

'We'll head to the tunnel now. Will the others come?' I asked. It seemed that the more witches we had, the easier it would be to protect Mary Jane from Samuel.

'No, it's best if we split up,' Jemima said, then turned to the remaining witches. 'You lot, stay behind and protect the house with vervain.'

'Vervain won't work,' Damon said flatly. 'He's immune.'

Jemima nodded once. 'All right then. I'll leave it to you to come up with something else. Maybe the *impervio* spell. The protective spell,' she added for our benefit. 'But if he's after Mary Jane, I doubt he'll stay around once he realises she's not here.'

'I can do that spell,' Vivian said uncertainly, as though convincing herself. Her face had drained of colour. Billy, on the other hand, had risen to his full height and pushed his shoulders back, as if to show his strength was a match for Samuel's.

'I'll come back each day to check in. I'm sure we'll have a plan to defeat Samuel soon,' Jemima said matter-of-factly. A shiver ran up my spine. Involving the witches meant even more lives were at stake, and we were past the point where running away was an option. Soon, someone would be dead. And I only hoped it would be Samuel – not one of us.

We made our way out of the house and emerged into sunlight. I pulled out my pocket watch. It was two o'clock. We'd slept for hours.

Silently, we walked along the Thames towards the tunnel. The docks weren't nearly as sinister in daylight as they were at night. Now, instead of being ghostly quiet, they were crammed with girls selling flowers, vendors hawking meat pies and sailors jockeying for work. We easily blended in with the masses, and I was glad for it.

Cora fell into pace with Damon, and Mary Jane walked beside me, although none of us spoke. Jemima trailed behind us. All I could do was stare at the rippling water, wondering where Violet's body had come to rest.

We got to the tunnel, and Cora hustled Mary Jane and Jemima over to start the fire for a cup of tea. I think Cora also sensed that Damon was holding back what he knew about

Samuel's quest for a purebred witch. With Mary Jane out of earshot, maybe he'd be more likely to talk.

'Are you sure Samuel wants Mary Jane? How would he know he had the right girl? The purebred witch could be anyone,' I said.

'He's already made five mistakes,' Damon said, arching an eyebrow. 'But somehow, I think Mary Jane's heightened power is a pretty big clue, don't you agree, brother?'

I ignored him and walked over to tend to the fire, using old newspapers that Cora and I had collected. One of the pages caught my attention.

RIPPER RESPITE? read the headline, written in bold capital letters. It was followed by a line drawing of Damon. I skimmed the article.

'I'm committed to finding the beast and killing him,' says Samuel Mortimer, a generous benefactor of East End charity initiatives and a front-runner in the election for councillor for the City of London. 'Or else, rest assured, the beast will kill us.' Mortimer is not alone in this sentiment. Scotland Yard, the Metropolitan Police Force and the Whitechapel Vigilance Committee are all working around the clock to catch the killer.

I crumpled the paper and threw it onto the fire. I watched

the flickering flames, wishing some sort of clue for how to fight Samuel would appear. But there was only smoke.

'I've been thinking,' Damon said, lowering his voice to a whisper more quiet than the crackling fire. 'Should we speak to James?'

'I'm not sure if that's a good idea,' I said, glancing meaningfully at Cora. Jemima was eyeing us suspiciously. 'James is a merchant who sells to vampires *and* witches. We don't know where his loyalties lie; he might not be trustworthy. Besides, last time he sent us to Ephraim, and we have witches of our own now.'

'Plus, with Ephraim, we had to pay a price,' Cora piped up, turning to us from the fire.

'I gave him my blood,' I admitted. Before he would tell us where Violet was staying, Ephraim had demanded a vial of my blood as payment. At the time, I'd been so desperate that I'd given it gladly, but now I feared I'd been too hasty. After all, if a witch's heart was in such high demand, could it be possible that vampire blood also had its own nefarious purposes? I wasn't sure, and I hoped that I wouldn't come to regret having given mine to him.

'I turn my back on you for one week, and that's what you do?' Damon asked, raising his voice. 'We're vampires, brother. We *take* blood. We aren't supposed to give it away.'

Jemima cackled in the corner, but the laughter didn't

break the tension. 'What would you have done?' I asked irritably.

'I don't know. But I'd have thought twice before giving my blood to a raven-toting lunatic.'

'You never think twice. You'd probably have lunged at him with your fangs out and got into even worse trouble. Created another mess that I'd have to clean up,' I said.

'You were quite the fighter yesterday,' Damon noted.

'Thanks,' I said stiffly. Damon and I didn't do well when we spoke earnestly, and usually all it took was one misinterpreted statement to ignite a quarrel that would last for days.

'I don't like the sound of Ephraim. There has to be another powerful witch in London,' Damon said. 'Jemima, for one,' he added gallantly, nodding at her.

'Thank you for the compliment, but I'm only here to protect Mary Jane. And I don't do dark magic if I can help it.' Jemima shook her head and shivered. Despite her tough exterior, it was clear she was just like the rest of us: terrified and completely out of her element.

'Well, there has to be *someone* who can help us. Everyone in London brags that this city is the finest and most sophisticated in the world, and I assume that includes its witch population,' Damon said, as if finding a witch was as easy as finding a fine wine.

'Actually,' Mary Jane said hesitantly, 'there may be someone who can help us.' All four of us swivelled towards her. She looked pensive and sat resting her elbows on her knees. She reminded me a little bit of Anna, the daughter of Pearl, the apothecary in Mystic Falls. Both Pearl and Anna had been vampires and had always been so worried that people would discover their secret. I couldn't help but wonder if that was Mary Jane's fear, too.

'Besides your housemates?' I asked. If Mary Jane knew such powerful witches, why did she choose to live in a rotting slum with the other teenage orphans?

She nodded. 'I met my first witch when I was a child, only about eight or nine. I was living in an orphanage on Crouch End Row. It was rough place, and they worked us hard. The only times we'd ever have a break were when people came, looking to adopt us. Then the nuns who ran it would be as sweet as could be.' She laughed bitterly. 'They loved showing us off. We'd perform, almost as if we were trained animals. We'd recite poetry and say prayers and do anything we could to get ourselves chosen. Except I knew no one would want me. People thought I was strange, with my eyes and the way I talked to animals. So mostly, I just kept to myself.' She paused, lost in her own memories. 'I enjoyed playing with the squirrels out in the courtyard, making them do tricks, that kind of thing. I was usually so careful, ensuring no one saw. But one day, a woman caught me. The surprising part was that she wasn't shocked,' Mary Jane said in wonderment.

'What did she do?' I asked, caught up in the story.

'She laughed. And then she sat next to me and asked me if I could make the squirrel stand on its hind legs. So I asked it to, and it did. And then she said she could do it, too.' She sighed. 'Her name is Alice, and she's the Viscountess of Cardiganshire. Her husband is Lord Lowson. She said she wanted to adopt me.'

'And?' Cora asked.

'She lied,' Jemima said flatly.

'Jemima's heard the story many times,' Mary Jane said apologetically. 'But it's true. She visited every week and told me stories about what it would be like when I moved in with her. I'd have my own room and as many animals as I wanted. I'd have a home. But then it was finally the day that she was supposed to come to collect me. I waited by the gate, and she never came. Not that day nor the next day nor the next. Finally, the nuns who ran the orphanage told me she wasn't coming. And after that, I stopped even wanting to be adopted. So I stuck with Jemima. As soon as we could, we went out to the streets, and eventually met Billy and all them. They're my family now.'

I looked at Mary Jane, unsure how useful this information

would be. Alice had promised Mary Jane a life of luxury, only to yank it away. And if she could so callously break a promise to a child, how could we trust her now?

'Alice is just proof that not all witches are loyal to their own kind. We learned early that we should never trust anyone. It's not a bad lesson to learn,' Jemima said bluntly.

'So the question is, where is Lady Alice now?' Damon asked urgently.

Mary Jane shrugged. 'She's in the society pages all the time. She and her husband just had a Midsummer's Ball. The papers took pictures. She lives near Regent's Park, on Oval Road. I can take you to her,' Mary Jane said.

'You'll just be disappointed again,' Jemima said. 'Why do we need her?'

'I've been waiting for a reason to contact her. Whether she likes it or not, she owes me. And now's my time to cash in,' Mary Jane said, her lips flattening into a straight line.

'And if she doesn't agree?' Jemima pressed.

'Then we're no worse off than we are now,' Mary Jane said bitterly. 'I'm being targeted by a murderous vampire. I need to try whatever I can. And if you can't help me without being rude, than you should stay at home.'

The two girls faced each other down, and Jemima was the first to look away.

'Fine,' Jemima said. 'Let's go.'

CHAPTER 7

We climbed out of the tunnel and into the sunlight. I shivered. Despite the bright sky, it was a colder day than any in recent memory, and I even saw a few small, white snowflakes swirling about in the sky.

Cora slipped her small, cold hand in mine and I squeezed it. I liked taking care of her. It made me feel as if maybe, in some small way, I was making this entire nightmarish experience better for her. The city was bustling as usual, and it didn't take long for us to cross through the busy streets towards Knightsbridge. From there, the thoroughfares were broader and better swept. Instead of vendors and flower girls hawking their wares on the corner, hansom cabs crowded the kerb, eager to pick up one of the many groups of well-dressed women toting parcels from Harrods.

Mary Jane walked in front, leading the way to Lady Alice's house. As I followed, lost in my thoughts, everything started to make sense. Of course Samuel would seek his prey in the East End and pay special attention to the Magdalene Asylum. He was clearly hoping that the purebred witch he'd traced hadn't moved far from her birthplace. And he'd been right. Anger at Lady Alice sliced through my stomach. If she'd just adopted Mary Jane as promised, then Mary Jane would never have been in this position. Her refusal to do so was like signing a death warrant. I'd do everything I could to ensure that wasn't true.

'We're almost at Lady Alice's house. Now, follow my lead and let me do the talking,' Mary Jane said nervously, arching an eyebrow at Jemima.

'I'll try. All I want is to look out for you,' Jemima said.

'You too, Damon,' Mary Jane said. 'It's important we present a united front.'

'Yes, ma'am!' Damon said sarcastically. I didn't bother to shush him. For better or worse, the old Damon was back.

'House' was an understatement for the sprawling Georgian mansion that stood in front of us. It was set back from the road, surrounded by acres of greenery, as though it were a private park. A twelve-foot-tall wrought-iron fence wrapped around the property. Its spiked top was garlanded with twisting rose vines, an attempt to make it less forbidding. Now, however, they had yet to be cut back for winter, and the brown, flowerless stems looked ugly and ominous.

Mary Jane didn't even pause at the grand sight and marched up the winding slate path to the front entrance. In the distance, I could see the stables, and beyond that, the expanse of Regent's Park. When I'd come to London, the park had been all lush green grass and a canopy of trees. Now ghostly bare branches dotted the landscape, and the ground was covered with brown leaves.

Mary Jane rapped on the front door. Almost immediately the door swung open, revealing a dour woman with white hair pulled back in a tight bun.

'Is Lady Alice expecting you?' Disgust was stamped on her face as she looked Mary Jane up and down.

'No, she's not. But please tell her that Mary Jane Kelly is here for her. She'll know who it is.'

'Mary Jane Kelly?' the woman asked. 'And what about the rest of you lot?'

'Just tell her that Mary Jane's here. I'll explain the rest,' she said firmly.

'All right,' the maid sighed. 'I'll see if my missus wants to see you,' she said, turning on her heel and closing the door firmly behind her.

Mary Jane turned towards us. 'She'll remember me. She *has* to,' she said, as if convincing herself.

I clenched my jaw, wondering what would happen when

Lady Alice came to the door and realised Mary Jane wasn't alone. I knew it wouldn't take long for Lady Alice to realise Damon and I were vampires. I wasn't sure whether they could smell the blood on our hands or sense our nature some other way, but the witches knew.

Before I had time to allow all the what-if scenarios to unravel in my mind, a woman wearing a gauzy white dress opened the door, her blonde curls piled on top of her head. I blinked. She was beautiful in an otherworldly way, like the angels depicted in stained-glass cathedral windows. Her eyelashes were golden-white and her skin sparkled as though it had been dusted with finely crushed diamonds. It was impossible to tell her age, although I assumed, from what Mary Jane had told us, she had to be well into her forties.

'Mary Jane, it's really you!' she cried, pulling Mary Jane to her and tightly hugging her as she rocked back and forth. Then she stepped back and appraised us, her eyes glittering.

She sucked in her breath as she glanced between Damon and me.

'Mary Jane, what are you doing with those men?' she hissed. 'Don't you know what they are?'

'They're helping me,' Mary Jane said, anger edging her voice. 'I need people I can count on.'

'After everything that happened, you owe Mary Jane, and

you know it,' Jemima piped up.

Confusion crossed Lady Alice's face. 'I wanted to adopt you, Mary Jane, I really did. But the day I was supposed to pick you up, I received word that my husband, who was fighting the war in Africa, was injured. I dropped everything to be by his side. I sent a message to the orphanage that I would be back for you when we had a more stable home. But by the time I went back to the orphanage to fetch you, you were gone.'

'Really?' Mary Jane asked.

'Yes!' Lady Alice said passionately.

'I never knew any of that,' Mary Jane said in a small voice.

'You know I'm telling the truth,' Lady Alice said meaningfully. Behind us, Jemima coughed sarcastically.

Lady Alice directed her attention to Jemima. 'I'm being honest, and you know it. We're cut from the same cloth, and I want to help you, just as I want to help Mary Jane. But first, tell me, why are you here now? Why did you bring vampires to my doorstep?'

She glanced at our group, allowing her gaze to rest on each of us. I wanted to believe her. But no matter what she said, she wasn't obligated to Mary Jane, and from the hateful looks she gave Damon and me, I wasn't sure she'd help Mary Jane if it also meant helping us. I had to say something.

'Stefan Salvatore, ma'am,' I said. *No lying*, I reminded

myself. 'And yes, we are helping Mary Jane. A dangerous vampire is after her heart, and we're doing the best we can to protect her. But we need your help. Know that we come here with nothing but good intentions.'

'After her heart?' Lady Alice murmured in concern.

'Yes. I was attacked down by the docks, and Stefan saved me,' Mary Jane explained.

Lady Alice stepped back as though she'd been struck by an unseen hand. 'Who attacked you? Tell me everything.'

'Samuel Mortimer, ma'am,' I said. 'He's—'

'Next in line to be London's councillor. Of course. Of course.' Lady Alice said, blinking several times in quick succession. Finally, she placed her hand over her mouth to compose herself. 'Samuel Mortimer? Why, we've been to his house. We've been to the Continent with him. Are you saying that—'

'Yes,' Damon said, seething with impatience. 'He's a vampire, and no one's noticed. Not even you.'

'Well, he must have some powerful magic on his side,' Lady Alice said, ignoring Damon's rude remark. 'But I'm powerful, too. And I can protect Mary Jane. It's the least I can do after all these years. Come,' she said, putting her hand on Mary Jane's shoulder and urging her inside.

'Wait!' I called. 'You need to let us in, too. We may be vampires, but we're committed to destroying Samuel.

That's why we're here. Cora, too. He turned her sister into a vampire.'

Lady Alice whirled round, her lips set in a firm line. 'Why should I help you? I'm thankful you saved Mary Jane, but I don't see how getting involved in a battle with a vampire would benefit me.'

'You don't have a choice,' Jemima said, stepping in front of us. 'I'm involved, and so are three other witches. Whether you like it or not, this is a war. And Samuel will think nothing of going after anyone connected to Mary Jane if he thinks it would help him. He's done his research. As someone who was planning to adopt Mary Jane, I'm sure your name appears in some of the ledgers,' Jemima added, as if issuing a challenge. 'It wouldn't take much for him to come after you, too.'

'She's right. And Stefan and I know how Samuel works. We'll be helping you as much as you're helping us. And we all want to help Mary Jane,' Damon said, taking a step closer to Alice. His foot toed the entrance to the hall and I knew we were both wondering how we could possibly get Alice to invite us in.

'Well, let's talk,' she said reluctantly. She stepped into the portico and closed the door behind her. 'Not inside. You understand, I'm sure,' she said. Her dress was a thin silk and the sleeves were sheer lace, yet she didn't seem cold, despite the chill. She wasn't wearing shoes or stockings either, the clearest sign that she wasn't at all a typical lady of London.

'I'm afraid I can't offer any of you a drink. Especially not the beverages you boys enjoy,' she called over her shoulder as she glided through the grass. It was almost as if her feet didn't touch the ground. She led us past the stables to a small hill. A rose-covered trellis covered its top. Unlike the vines adorning the fence, these were in full bloom and bursting with red and pink blossoms, despite the season. A small well surrounded by low stone benches sat beneath them.

'This is one of my favourite places. Please, sit,' she said, gesturing to the benches. I sat opposite her, and Cora slid into place beside me. Mary Jane sat between Lady Alice and Jemima. Damon, rather than sitting, leaned against the well.

Several sparrows flew over to perch on the wooden roof of the well, chirping quizzically. I thought back to the story of Mary Jane and the rat and wondered if the birds were speaking to Lady Alice. I suddenly wished my past hadn't included a diet quite so heavy on sparrows.

'Now,' Lady Alice said urgently, leaning forward. 'I know Mary Jane wouldn't take the decision to consort with vampires lightly. And I doubt vampires would want to consort with witches, even if a life is in danger,' she said, emphasising the word *vampire* in the same way she'd inflect *dung beetle* or *lunatic*. 'This is about more than just Mary Jane's well-being.'

'No!' I protested loudly.

'It is. Vampires never do anything unless it will benefit them. It's the way you are, part of nature, same as the trees losing their leaves in autumn.' She crossed her arms and appraised us critically.

'Partially,' I admitted. 'The Ripper is Samuel Mortimer. He's framing Damon and trying to kill us both.'

'And he's *still* after me. I was able to hold him off, and they were able to wound him, but he'll be back,' Mary Jane said. 'Damon says it's because he's looking for the heart of a purebred witch. Is that true? Do you know who I am?'

'I never knew for certain, but I had suspicions,' Lady Alice said. 'Your eyes, for one. I've seen a few powerful witches with eyes like yours. But that wasn't why I wanted to adopt you,' she added quickly. 'I'm so glad you're safe, and that you're here. I'll do anything to save you. Even if it does mean working with vampires,' she said finally.

'How does everyone but me know I'm a purebred witch?' Mary Jane asked.

Lady Alice sighed. 'You have so much to learn, my dear. I could sense you were special, just like I knew these two were vampires. And Samuel must only have rumours to go on, which is why he was ripping apart any girl who seemed to vaguely fit your description. The only real way to find a purebred witch is to see her heart, which shimmers gold instead of red. That's why the Ripper – Samuel – has been hacking his victims to pieces.'

Of course. The knife wounds, the innards torn from the chest . . . the gruesome murders all made sense. Samuel wasn't simply trying to shock London with his murders – he was on a mission that we couldn't even have imagined.

'It kind of gives a new meaning to the term "heartsick", doesn't it?' Damon quipped.

I glared at him. Then I glanced over at Mary Jane. Her trembling lower lip was the only sign that she was terrified.

'So, do you have any idea who my parents are?' Mary Jane asked.

Lady Alice shook her head sadly. 'I'm afraid I don't. But I do know that all the nuns at the orphanage thought you were a miracle baby. You were placed on the doorstep on the coldest night of the year, and yet, when they found you the next morning, your body was warm. That was powerful magic coursing through your veins,' she said. 'You must somehow be related to a member of the Original coven. It's our secret history, but Samuel has obviously done his research.'

'But why?' Damon interrupted angrily. 'What's so special about some witch?'

'You must be a young vampire,' she said, snorting in disgust. 'How old are you? Two years? And don't call me ma'am. It makes me sound ancient.'

'We both turned in 1864,' I said quickly, before Damon could butt in with a caustic comment.

'I see. Well, there are many reasons why a power-crazed vampire would want a witch. But there's only one reason a vampire would want a purebred heart.'

'Why?' Mary Jane asked in a whisper, as though she were afraid to hear the answer.

'I can't go further until I have some security.' Lady Alice's gaze flicked to us, then landed on Jemima. 'Do you know how to do a loyalty spell?' she asked. It was the first time she'd acknowledged Jemima in a while, and Jemima seemed taken aback.

'A simple one, yes,' she said meekly.

'Good. Can you perform it between the two vampires and me?'

'All right.' Jemima exhaled, and I could tell she was nervous at her skills being put to the test. 'I need a lock of hair from each of you.'

I reached to the top of my head and plucked a few strands for her. Lady Alice and Damon did the same. She squinted at them and braided them together, her brow furrowed. The braid thickened and grew until it became a multicoloured rope.

'Put out your hands. Palms up, please,' she said. Then she took the rope and tied it loosely on each of our wrists. *'Fidelitas ad finum!'* She clapped her hands. The rope disappeared, but left a shiny red welt against my skin. Damon and Lady Alice had similar ones. It throbbed in time with my heart.

'We're bound. Thank you,' Lady Alice said, as though Jemima had performed a task as simple as pouring a cup of coffee. 'That spell means that even if you wanted to betray me, you couldn't. The words wouldn't be able to escape from your lips. And now I can tell you all I know.'

'Please do,' I said.

'Legend is, if a vampire eats the heart of a purebred witch, he can compel other vampires,' Lady Alice said sadly. She reached to drape her arm over Mary Jane's shoulders, but Mary Jane jerked away, holding both hands to her chest as she lurched from the bench and began to run.

'I don't believe any of this!' she yelled from halfway across the garden. 'You're trying to scare me!'

'Mary Jane, it's all right!' Cora ran towards her and pulled her into an embrace.

'But it's not all right!' Mary Jane said, her voice muffled as she buried her face in Cora's shoulder. 'If he can do that with my heart, that means he'll never, ever leave me alone.

And even if we *do* kill Samuel, then what if another vampire wants to kill me? I'll never be safe!'

'*Shh*, there, there,' Lady Alice said. 'You will be safe. Stay with me. We're safe here. If you're here, you'll have nothing to worry about.'

We needed Lady Alice, and although I knew she'd do whatever it took to help Mary Jane, I wasn't sure complete her loyalty extended to us. If Mary Jane decided to stay in Lady Alice's mansion, how would we convince them to work with us to trap Samuel?

I rested a hand on Mary Jane's back to comfort her, only to have Lady Alice shoot me a look. I snatched my hand away.

'We're keeping Mary Jane safe,' I explained awkwardly.

'They've been protecting me, too,' Cora piped up. I shot her a grateful look.

'Where?' Lady Alice asked crisply.

'Near the Bank of London,' I said evasively, not wanting to give away the fact that our current address was a tunnel far below ground.

'*Near* the bank? But where exactly, pray tell?' she asked quizzically, knitting her eyebrows together. I wasn't being compelled. I was entirely in charge of my own faculties, and yet the knowledge that I *couldn't* lie set me on edge.

'An Underground tunnel,' I admitted.

Lady Alice shook her head. 'Two grown-up vampires might belong underground. And as for the human girl, well, whoever she decides to spend her time with is her own foolish choice. I don't interfere with humans unless absolutely necessary. But, Mary Jane, I insist you stay here. Your friend can, too,' she said, nodding at Jemima.

Mary Jane pulled back. 'No. I know you mean well, but it would be too hard to stay here now. I wanted more than anything to live with you when I was little. Now I'm used to being on my own. I need to stay with Stefan and Damon. I trust them. And they need me,' she said in a small, proud voice.

Lady Alice pursed her lips as if to protest, but then nodded once. 'Very well. But I'm involved now and I'm not going to let you disappear from my life again. We'll take the matter to my coven. You know what a coven is, don't you, Mary Jane?' she asked as if she were a schoolteacher.

'I . . . I think so,' Mary Jane said uncertainly.

Lady Alice clucked her tongue against the roof of her mouth. 'You have so much to learn. I hate that this is how we've come together again, but trust me, your life will change for the better. And there's no need for you to stay in that tunnel. You can stay with me and still help your vampire friends. But from a distance. The way it should be.'

'They're not my "vampire friends",' Mary Jane said in a

93

low voice. 'They're Stefan and Damon. They're good men.'

'They're not men at all,' Lady Alice said. 'These vampires might be better than most, but I want you to know that, beyond this challenge, we can't really trust them. They're monsters.'

'Will you stop?' Damon interrupted loudly. 'I'm so *sick* of it. It was the same bloody thing in the Civil War, where soldiers wouldn't trust one another because so-and-so's grandfather was from Massachusetts, so Northern blood was in his veins. Well, we're all monsters, and we're all misfits. I'm here, and I'm ready to get involved in your spell-casting, but I won't do it if I'm going to be mocked and mistrusted.'

Lady Alice's eyes flashed. 'I've been around just as long as you, Damon. I could tell you horrible stories about the war between vampires and witches, and they wouldn't even scratch the surface of why I hate your species,' she said as she turned to the well and let down a tiny wooden pail into the blackness below. The well itself looked like it belonged in a museum, perhaps in an exhibit about the lives of fifteenth-century villagers.

'Would the both of you stop arguing?' Jemima interrupted. 'I don't care what you call each other, but I think Mary Jane should stay with Lady Alice. It's safer. Stefan, Samuel knows you saved her. If we both stay with Alice instead, there's a smaller chance he can find us here.'

'Of course,' Lady Alice said coolly. She pulled the bucket back up and held it towards Mary Jane. Liquid sloshed out of it. 'Drink some,' she said. 'It'll help protect you. Protect – but not save. All this water does is surround you with goodwill and thoughts. Don't think it gives you licence to do anything foolish.'

'Goodwill from the well?' Damon quipped. 'Why not charge for it?'

Lady Alice glared at him. 'It's not for you to understand,' she said crisply.

'Or to drink,' he said under his breath as Lady Alice passed the bucket to Mary Jane.

'Thank you,' Mary Jane said, and drank deeply, water running down her chin. I wondered whether the water really was magic. For her sake, I hoped so.

For *all* our sakes, I hoped so.

'Thank you for your kindness,' I echoed, even though Lady Alice hadn't been especially kind to us.

The wind had picked up and the sparrows perching on the well's roof scattered. I watched them fly above us, tiny brown dots against the light-grey sky, and I remembered the mysterious meeting Cora and I had had with Ephraim. He'd had a raven that responded to his beck and call. Did Lady Alice have a special kinship with these sparrows? With witches, nothing was what it seemed. Even if we were bound in loyalty to Lady Alice, what did that mean? And how would I know whether or not to trust her coven?

'We'll meet tomorrow at midnight. I'll be waiting in Kensington Gore to collect you. Don't be late or my fellow witches may be even less inclined to help you vampires than usual.'

'Kensington *Gore*?' Damon interrupted.

A shadow of a smile, the first I'd seen from her, appeared on Lady Alice's face. 'Yes. The coven thinks it's rather amusing, too. It's just the name of the street, not some occult ritual. It's right by the Royal Albert Hall, where we hold our meetings. Come alone, without candles, stakes or any other weapons. And be prepared to follow the orders of the coven.' She walked over to me and grabbed my shirt, pulling me towards her with a firm tug.

'Promise that no matter what, you'll do everything in your power to see that no harm comes to Mary Jane. Do I have your word?'

'You have my word,' I said, each syllable as deliberate and heavy as an anvil.

'Good.' Lady Alice clapped her hands and the wind died down at once, scattering leaves all over the benches on which we'd been sitting. 'I'll see you tomorrow night. I'll leave you to let yourselves out,' she said, nodding slightly. 'And remember, we haven't agreed to anything. But I want to be fair and give you a chance to petition my coven in person. You'll ask them for vinculum. If they agree, then we'll go forward. And if they don't, then the matter is out of my hands.'

'Vinculum?' I asked.

Lady Alice nodded crisply. 'A bonding spell. Under its terms, two warring groups are bound together. Only a murder by the other side destroys the spell. It's a bond created so one side may not turn on the other.'

'Is there a reason it can't be invoked right now? After all, we're here. We trust you. We've already performed the loyalty spell.'

She shook her head. 'It's not that simple. That spell simply makes it impossible for either party to reveal any secrets that might be harmful to the other. But vinculum requires each side to agree to put aside their own interests and fight for a common cause. While vampires tend to work on their own, witches are strongest in groups. If my coven agrees, you'll have their entire support behind you.'

'And if they don't?' Damon interrupted.

'Then I'm afraid I won't be able to help you. Of course, I'll still protect Mary Jane, but you won't be part of our plan of action,' Lady Alice said in a matter-of-fact tone.

As if to underscore her point, the well began to rumble. Blue and red shoots of water erupted from the opening.

'Quite a magic show. And to think, we didn't even have to pay a penny,' Damon joked.

'Damon!' I admonished. But the faintest trace of a smile crossed Lady Alice's face.

'Mark my words, you haven't seen anything yet, vampire,' she said. 'If my coven decides to help you, you'll witness things beyond your wildest dreams.'

CHAPTER 8

'Do you think this is a trap?' Cora murmured as we crept along Kensington Gore, near the Royal Albert Hall. As if on cue, Big Ben chimed far off in the distance. The three of us were exactly in the spot Lady Alice had appointed us to meet. It was midnight, and Lady Alice – and, for that matter, Mary Jane or Jemima – was nowhere to be seen. On my wrist, the red welt from the loyalty spell throbbed.

'No.' I sounded more confident than I felt. When I heard the witches convened in the Royal Albert Hall, I imagined it to be a theatre much like the West End music hall Violet and I had visited back when she was a human. But this building took my breath away. It was a domelike structure surrounded by windows on all sides, with many tiers that made it look like an enormous wedding cake.

'It's not a trap.' A smooth voice made me jump. I whirled round. Lady Alice was standing behind us, as though she'd been there the whole time. She was wearing a simple black dress and a diamond clip was holding her hair at her neck. She looked like she was about to go to the opera. Mary Jane was behind her, clad in a white dress with her hair pinned back in a similar diamond clip.

'So what is it then, a party game?' Damon asked sarcastically, clearly not impressed by Lady Alice's sudden appearance.

'No, the coven doesn't play games. We trust each other,' she said, ignoring Damon. 'Terrible things happen when that trust is broken.'

'Terrible things happen when vampires turn on each other, too, but that doesn't stop them,' Damon said darkly.

'Well, that's another reason why we're better than you, isn't it?' she said crisply. 'Now, come. Everyone's already gathered. I'll leave it to you both to explain what you need.'

'Where's Jemima?' I whispered to Mary Jane as Lady Alice turned away. I hoped that Jemima and Lady Alice hadn't got into a disagreement.

'Checking on the others,' Mary Jane replied. She seemed more confident than I'd seen her before. I was happy that she and Lady Alice had finally reunited.

Without waiting for a response, Lady Alice pulled open a wooden trapdoor that lay between the cobblestones of the walkway. Despite the rusty chains giving it the appearance of being tightly locked, it creaked open.

The four of us followed Lady Alice into the darkness and onto a shaky iron spiral staircase that rattled with each footstep. A match blazed in her hand, casting shadows on the concrete walls. While the exterior of the Albert Hall was majestic, this wasn't. It was as cold and damp as the Underground tunnel we called home.

Finally, the staircase stopped.

'This is where the magic happens,' Lady Alice said as I took in our surroundings. Hallways containing racks of costumes, props and scenery branched out in every direction from where we stood. Directly opposite the spiral staircase we'd just descended was a set of twelve steps that led to nowhere. Clearly, it was a prop for a stage show.

Lady Alice walked to the side of the fake staircase and pushed open a flimsy wooden door.

'Go on,' she said, gesturing for me to walk through the door. I blinked. It was pitch black and quiet inside. The door was only four feet high, and I had to duck to get through. I found myself standing in a dark coat closet.

But only for a moment.

Then, right before my eyes, the room began expanding. The ceiling vaulted, the walls fanned out and furniture appeared out of nowhere. And I realised I wasn't alone. Chatter surrounded me as the room brightened with orange light. Two white marble benches flanked a fire. Three men and three women sat on the benches. Two of the men looked ancient. The other was middle-aged and had his fingers interlaced with those of a well-dressed woman. An elderly woman perched on a stool by the door, while a girl, scarcely older than Mary Jane, sat apart from the others, on the very edge of a bench. Who were these people? And how did they all find one another? And, most important, would they agree to help us?

I heard someone come through the doorway behind me. 'Does she have to turn everything into a damn magic trick?' Damon whispered under his breath, so low only I could hear it.

'Shh!' I was comforted by the untraditional entrance. It was reassuring to have evidence of Lady Alice's skills before I put my faith in her.

'I hope you didn't have too much trouble getting in,' a wizened man said as he hurried over to Damon. 'Of course, I knew who you were from those parties at White's, but I wasn't going to say anything. You seemed to be behaving yourself. But I have to admit, I'm glad to see you in this setting.' His gaze shifted to me. 'And another one!' he said as he grabbed my hand and shook it. I shifted uncomfortably and ran my tongue over my canine teeth.

Still short and straight. The man turned to our escort. 'All right, Alice. Now can you tell us why we're here?'

'Yes, Thatcher,' she said as she patted her hand on his hunched shoulder and subtly forced him back to the marble bench where he'd been sitting. 'Now, I've told you that we'd have guests tonight. Stefan, Damon and Mary Jane? Please, come forward.' She ushered us to a spot next to her in front of the fire. 'Cora, take a seat.'

Cora nodded nervously, sitting next to a beautiful young woman dressed in a blue velvet dress. Her long curls cascaded down her back and her neck and wrists were dripping with gold and jewels. The half-dozen people in the room looked like lords and ladies from the society pages. Nothing about their dress, or demeanour, revealed their true selves. I felt a pang of envy. They could live normal lives. They could blend in, without worrying about losing control or an accidental flash of fangs.

'As I'm sure all of you noticed, these men are not witches, but vampires,' Lady Alice continued, not bothering to introduce the witches in front of us. 'You'll also notice they're accompanied by one of our own tonight.' She turned and softened her gaze towards Mary Jane. 'This girl is Mary Jane Kelly, a very powerful witch who doesn't know the greatness of her gifts. She's descended from the Original coven,' she said, nodding as several witches in the room gasped.

'Why is a purebred witch wasting her time with ghastly

bloodsucking monsters?' The woman in the blue dress sniffed. Cora shot a dagger-like glare at her.

'Because one of us is the ghastly bloodsucking monster who saved her,' Damon said smoothly, smiling his cat-who-ate-the-canary smile.

Lady Alice nodded. 'It's true. Why don't you explain the rest?' she asked, looking expectantly at me.

I glanced around at the witches, trying to make eye contact. It was imperative they see me as their friend. But before I could explain that I was the one who'd saved Mary Jane, Damon continued.

'You may know me as Damon DeSangue, and this is my brother, Stefan. I came to your country a year ago, and I quickly made the acquaintance of London's elite, including Samuel Mortimer,' he intoned. 'But I can report to you with complete honesty that Samuel Mortimer is a vampire. *And* he's Jack the Ripper.'

'That's outrageous!' one of the old men blurted out, his head snapping up at the word *vampire*. 'I know Samuel Mortimer. He's a bloody great man.' A few dissenting grumbles echoed in the audience.

Cora came forward. 'It's true. He killed two of my friends and turned my sister into a vampire. I've seen him in the act, and I assure you he's the Ripper.'

'The girl's telling the truth,' one of the men stated,

verbalising what all the witches must have known.

'Samuel as the Ripper. I *knew* it,' one woman murmured. 'Didn't I tell you, Oscar?' She turned to the man on her left. 'Why, at one of Cecil's parties I straight-out asked Samuel if he had any leads. When he answered, I *knew* he was lying, but I thought he was covering up a secret Scotland Yard was keeping. I should have pushed him further,' she said, looking distraught as the man next to her patted her hand.

'Please, don't blame yourselves!' Damon said gallantly, a gleam of excitement evident in his blue eyes. Damon in front of a crowd was an impressive sight, and I knew he was just warming up. 'Samuel Mortimer began a reign of terror in the East End, not for sport but because he thought his killings would lead to the prize he covets.' At this, Damon lowered his voice so much that they had to lean in to hear him. 'He wants the heart of a purebred witch. And he's convinced that witch is Mary Jane.'

'It's true,' Lady Alice said. 'All of it.'

'What happens if he gets the heart?' the woman in the blue dress asked, leaning forward in concern.

'He's going to eat it.' The elderly woman by the door cut off Damon before he could answer. 'And by doing so, he will gain the power to compel vampires. He can get all the vampires in London to do his bidding.' She slid off her stool and hobbled towards us, leaning on an intricately carved wooden cane. 'But why should we help *them*? We can do this ourselves. How do we know they aren't just setting this up as a trap for this . . . this *Samuel*,' she spat, as if the name was the worst thing she could think to say. She glanced around the room indignantly, the eyebrows on her wrinkled, withered-apple face knitting together. Her strident tone reminded me of Mrs Duckworth, the housekeeper at Abbott Manor. She was the type of woman people listened to.

'My brother and I have witnessed first-hand the unspeakable horrors Samuel has committed. I assure you that we are dedicated to fighting him until he is stopped once and for all,' I interjected. 'As for taking care of yourselves, you may have magic, but Samuel is cunning and ruthless and therefore not to be underestimated. We've been following him for weeks,' I explained. 'We know his habits, and we know his weaknesses. We have strength, and we have knowledge of our enemy. While separately we might fail, by banding together we have a chance at ridding London of this fiend. And so we're humbly asking for vinculum to be invoked. Lady Alice told us about the spell, and it seems it's what we need. I know vampires and witches have a complicated history, but if we have a spell that binds us, then you won't have to fear us.'

The old woman nodded, but it was impossible to tell what she was thinking. She had the same strange pupils as

Mary Jane. They were captivating, and it was hard to tear my eyes away.

Please, I thought. I didn't dare say the word. But as I thought it, the woman's eyes flickered.

'I'm aware of what we're risking, Lavinia,' Lady Alice said gently to the old woman. 'But I'm also aware of the dangers in not binding ourselves to these vampires. Samuel will kill Mary Jane, and if he does, he could have all of London under his control. I won't take that chance. Mary Jane is one of our own. And we protect our own. Or have you forgotten that in your old age? What does the rest of the coven think?' she asked, not bothering to wait for Lavinia's response.

'I say kill the bloody bastard by any means necessary!' a portly, red-faced old man blustered. The men in the group murmured their agreement.

'I agree. Whatever we can do to save Mary Jane,' the young blonde woman in the front said shyly. I sneaked a glance at Mary Jane. She was staring at a point far in front of her. Her face was pale. Just because the witches were helping didn't mean she was out of danger, and she knew it.

'I don't think so.' Lavinia shook her head vehemently. 'These strangers come here in front of us, say they're vampires, and say that one of their own needs the heart of a purebred witch. Now, I know they seem to be telling the truth, but vampires are crafty. And before we go any further, we need the girl,' she said, beckoning to Cora.

'M-m-me?' Cora asked, stuttering in fear.

'No, the other human girl who was brought in front of our coven,' Lavinia growled sarcastically. 'Yes, *you*.'

Cora stepped forward, and I could see her shoulders trembling underneath her frayed dress.

'Now, Cora,' Lavinia said, staring straight into her eyes. 'Will you tell me the truth?' Her intensity reminded me of the way I focused before compelling. Cora's gaze flickered towards me.

'Cora!' Lavinia said, causing her gaze to snap forward.

'Yes?' Cora asked.

'When you open your mouth, will you speak the truth?' she asked again.

'Yes,' Cora said. There was no question in her voice. Lavinia placed one hand, then the other on her shoulders. She nodded to the coven.

'What will these vampires do once they've defeated Samuel?'

'I don't know,' Cora said in confusion, breaking her gaze.

Lavinia shook her shoulders. 'Well, think! Two vampires, able to compel themselves into any situation or station, would want to do *something*, wouldn't they? Maybe gain power? Riches? Rule the city of London?'

'Damon wouldn't. He wants an easy life. Whatever luxuries he can have, he'll get, but he won't cause trouble here. Not like Samuel. And Stefan—' She paused, and a small smile crossed her face. 'I think that if Stefan kills Samuel, then he'll finally stop feeling ashamed of who he truly is. He needs to do something good. Something heroic. But he won't cause trouble. I know that.'

These were clearly Cora's unedited thoughts. I felt she'd accurately pegged Damon, but I couldn't help but feel betrayed at what she'd said about me. *That* was why she thought I wanted to fight Samuel? So I could feel heroic? She didn't think it had to do with my wanting to save her?

'How interesting,' Lavinia said, breaking the silence. Her mouth twisted as though she'd sucked a lemon, and she took her hands off Cora. Cora staggered back as if she had been pushed.

'Are you all right?' Mary Jane asked, steadying Cora and helping her regain her balance.

She nodded, even though I saw her wince and rub her shoulder.

Lavinia turned to address the coven. 'I'm satisfied that these vampires are who they say. And I won't stand in the way of our affiliation with them.'

'Good,' Lady Alice said simply. 'Now, let's pledge vinculum. And then we'll formulate a plan. Stefan, please take my blood. Damon, you too.' She held her arms out towards us, her wrists facing the vaulted ceiling.

'Take your blood?' I repeated, hoping I'd misheard.

Lady Alice nodded briskly, not moving her arms. 'Yes. With your fangs, please. Vinculum happens when a witch freely gives her blood and a vampire freely accepts it. No spells, no compulsion, no lying. Just an honest exchange. You will be bound to me, and I'm bound to my coven. But again, if any deception occurs, or any lives are lost, vinculum is broken.'

'What happens if vinculum is broken?' Damon asked.

'It varies,' Lady Alice said smoothly. 'Broadly speaking, it means we have to face the wrath of the other species. All propriety and rules are forgotten, and we battle until we feel balance is restored. In this case, we'd kill you. And I assume you would kill us,' she said matter-of-factly.

'Seems fair.' Damon nodded, but I felt dread creep through my veins. The witches were brutal. If things didn't go according to plan, we'd suddenly have a powerful new enemy.

'Are we agreed, then?' Lady Alice asked as she pushed her wrist under my nose. Her skin smelled of gardenias and jasmine and I wanted so badly to taste the blood running underneath it. I staggered back.

'I can't. Damon will have to do it,' I said.

'All right,' Lady Alice said uncertainly, turning towards Damon.

'No.' I stared at Lavinia, who was shaking her head. 'Either both of them do it, or I won't allow this bond to happen. Why doesn't the vampire drink?'

'I don't drink human blood,' I mumbled. I'd always been proud of my resolve, but here, when blood was being offered, I felt weak. What if I couldn't stop at a sip? What if I ruined everything?

'Then how did you ever expect to fight this Samuel?' Lavinia asked, her eyes boring right into me. I glanced over to Cora, but she looked down at her hands folded in her lap. 'You said that you were bringing vampire strength to this battle. But if you're refusing blood, then you're refusing that strength within you,' Lavinia said.

'We only need one vampire to do it, right? Maybe it's better—'

'Not for me,' Lavinia said flatly. 'Either this vampire feeds on Alice's blood, or the deal is off.'

I looked at Cora, and she nodded encouragingly. Still, she didn't *truly* know what human blood did to me. In her mind, I was a wishful hero. She didn't know me as the monster who'd never, ever have his fill.

'Go on, brother,' Damon said. It was the same phrase he'd used to egg me on countless times, ever since I was a child and he'd dared me to jump off the Wickery Bridge on the first warm day of the year.

I didn't have a choice. I slowly pulled her wrist to my mouth. My fangs sliced into her skin, releasing the pungent, sweet smell of blood into the air. I plunged my canines into the tiny blue veins in her wrist and was hit with waves of ecstasy I hadn't felt in almost twenty years. I allowed the blood to wash down my throat, feeling it soothe all the pain and fear I'd carried. It surged through my body, making me feel safe and strong and alive. This was better than the blood in New Orleans, better than the oceans of blood I'd drunk during the murderous sprees of my youth.

Better than my father's blood.

I wanted more, as much as possible, enough to fill my veins and my heart. A growl escaped from my lips.

'Vampire!' Lavinia called sharply.

I pulled back and wiped my mouth. I felt all eyes on me.

'I'm sorry if I got carried away,' I said stiffly.

'You did exactly as I asked,' Lady Alice said, but her face was pale. 'Damon?'

She held out her wrist and I watched as Damon slowly took a small sip, as though he were drinking a fine champagne. I couldn't help but feel he was being so mannerly on purpose, to show the blood-hungry brother how proper feeding was done. I knew that even though

I'd drunk from Lady Alice's wrist only briefly, I'd revealed part of my true nature. I was too greedy, too insistent, and I'd heard my angry, guttural growl as clearly as everyone else had.

When Damon finished, Lady Alice brushed the excess blood away with the inside of her sleeve. 'Now, Damon and Stefan, come join our circle.' She held out her hands. Instead of standing next to her, I chose to stand between Damon and Lavinia. It seemed safer. Because now that the taste of her blood was on my tongue, it was all I could think about.

Lady Alice began to chant, and one by one the other witches joined in. I allowed my tongue to run back and forth over my teeth; the filmy coating left by the blood felt like both a blessing and a curse. The flames from the fire dimmed, sending the room into semi-darkness.

'Vinculum,' Lady Alice said. The rest of the witches echoed the word.

Vinculum, I said under my breath. I hoped it worked. It had to. Lavinia dropped my hand. The room brightened.

'It's done. We're bound,' Lady Alice said.

'Good. Now, let's discuss the next steps,' I said, glancing pointedly at Damon until he settled onto the bench next to the blonde-haired witch. 'What we need to do is trap Samuel, and the best way to do that is to use Mary Jane as bait. We can lead Samuel to her,' I said.

'How will you do that, vampire?' Lavinia asked.

'I thought we could have Samuel spot Mary Jane in the East End, then attack,' I explained.

'No, no, no!' Lavinia protested. 'Far too messy. We can't have the battle where humans are. We need to do it somewhere hidden.'

'My house,' Mary Jane said quietly. 'It's the perfect spot. We have a spell on the property that keeps the rent collectors away. Humans don't seem to notice it, even though it's right there.'

'Good thinking,' Lavinia said approvingly.

'I suppose one of *us* could be used to bait Samuel,' I suggested, thinking on the fly.

'Too dangerous.' Lavinia shook her head. 'Weren't you paying attention? Vampires are crafty. He'll kill you without thinking twice. You need Samuel to know you have something he wants. You need to tell him you have Mary Jane.'

'He already knows,' I said numbly.

'Does he know *he's* involved?' Lavinia asked, jerking her chin at Damon.

Damon shook his head.

'I say Damon goes and offers to bring Samuel to the girl,' one of the men suggested. 'I know Samuel, and he wants power. No matter what you've done to him, even if you've stared into his eyes as you've attempted to stake his chest, he'll forgive you, if it means he'll get what he wants.'

'All right.' Damon nodded. 'I can talk him into listening to me.' His eyes gleamed, and I knew if anyone could pretend he was going to the dark side, it was him.

'Damon will bring Samuel to Mary Jane, and we'll attack,' I said, finishing off the plan. The witches nodded in agreement. It seemed simple.

'Are there any spells that will protect her from a vampire? Vervain won't work. And Samuel has a witch on his side, so we need to protect against that, too,' I said, emboldened by the way the witches were agreeing with me.

'Who is the witch?' Lavinia asked.

'Seaver. He's the groundskeeper at the Magdalene Asylum.'

'Don't worry about *him*,' Lavinia said with a derisive wave. 'Stefan, you can take him on. He's not as powerful as you. All you need to do, *if* he appears, is simply kill him. A knife to the heart will do the trick.'

'All right.' I nodded. I'd killed before. I could kill again.

'And now, on to the most important thing. Protecting Mary Jane,' Lady Alice prodded.

'Should we do praesidium?' the middle-aged witch suggested.

'Not a bad idea,' the man next to her said.

'Praesidium is ideal,' Lady Alice agreed. 'Of course, it's not foolproof, and it's putting Mary Jane right on the front line. As her guardian, I wonder—'

'You're not my guardian,' Mary Jane said. 'I'm a grown woman. I can make my own decision. What exactly is praesidium?'

'A protection spell,' Lavinia said. 'It will make Mary Jane's body impenetrable to a vampire's touch. It's like a shield, but one that causes tremendous pain to a vampire if he touches it. The pain isn't fatal, but it will momentarily stun or surprise him. That way, the spell is twofold. It will protect Mary Jane from Samuel's clutches, and it will—'

'Allow us to attack,' I finished. 'That sounds perfect.'

Lady Alice nodded. 'It seems the best spell under the circumstances.'

'I'll do it,' Mary Jane said resolutely.

'Good.' I nodded at her. 'Damon will let Samuel know he has Mary Jane. He'll tell Samuel to come to us two nights from now, sending him right into the trap. We'll meet at five at Miller's Court and perform the spell before he comes. And then we'll be waiting for him.'

The blonde witch waved her hand up at me as though she were a schoolgirl and I were the teacher. 'All of us?' she asked.

I glanced round the group. It was small, but the room was tiny. 'Do we need everyone for the spell?' I asked.

Lady Alice shook her head. 'It's very simple.'

'Good. Then no, not everyone should be there. Just Mary Jane, Lady Alice and Lavinia in the house, and the rest in the alley, waiting as back-up if the plan doesn't work. But it will,' I said, reassuring myself as much as the witches.

Ten storeys above, I heard the lone, singular *caw* of a raven. The sound echoed in my ears, and I knew it was foreshadowing *something*. I only wished I knew what.

'I'll be there, vampire,' Lavinia said finally.

I locked eyes with her. 'Good,' I said. I meant it. Whether we liked it or not, we were bound to the witches. And they were bound to us.

CHAPTER 9

The next night, I was hiding in the bushes that surrounded the fence of Samuel's Lansdowne House estate. A few hundred paces away, Damon hunched in the shadows of one of the large portico columns of the Georgian mansion.

He turned towards me and I nodded to him. I was ready in case things went sour and he needed back-up.

He knocked on the door and was unsurprised when, seconds later, Samuel himself answered. His eyes were bloodshot, and his pale skin was almost white.

The wind had picked up and was blowing towards me, making it sound like the conversation was taking place only inches away.

'Listen. I'm here to offer you a deal,' Damon said stiffly, before Samuel could say anything – or stake him. 'A business transaction. From one *vampyr* to another,' he said, using the ancient, foreign-sounding term for one of our kind.

'A deal,' Samuel repeated. An inscrutable expression – was it amusement? Curiosity? Anger? – flickered across his face. 'You killed my brother. I ruined you. And yet, now you come to me to try to negotiate. Why?'

I held my breath, lest Samuel should hear me. Watching my brother talk calmly with a man hell-bent on destroying our lives, it was all I could do to sit back on my heels and stay quiet. Maybe it was the eleuthro from a few days ago or Lady Alice's blood, but something had changed within me. My nerves were on edge and I was ready to spring into battle at a second's notice. After all, the next few hours wouldn't merely determine Damon's and my fates – they would determine the fate of the entire city. In the words of my brother when he had a particularly good hand of poker: we were all-in. But right now, there was nothing I could do but watch the scene unfold.

Damon shifted back and forth on his feet, and I knew he was exercising every ounce of his self-control not to lash out and attack Samuel.

Say it. Damon's head jerked back to glance in my direction, even though I hadn't said the words out loud. *Admit he's won.*

'When I was a human, I was a soldier in the Confederate Army,' Damon said through gritted teeth. 'I know the difference between victory and defeat, and I know when to wave the white flag. I'm done fighting. I just want to make a deal, one man to another. Give me my life, my freedom, and I'll give you something you want,' he said, bowing slightly.

Samuel threw back his head and laughed, looking like a wolf baying at the moon. 'What could you *possibly* have that I want?'

'Your purebred witch,' Damon responded.

Samuel stepped towards him, slamming him against a column. I cringed as Damon's skull hit the plaster, leaving a lightning-bolt-shaped crack in the plaster. 'How do you know about that?' Samuel asked, emphasising each word.

Damon shrugged, seemingly unperturbed by the violent outburst. 'I overheard you and your minions discussing your search for a purebred witch. Stefan has Mary Jane. And now, thanks to his foolish rescue, I know exactly where she lives. She's defenceless and gullible. It'll be easy for me to get her for you.'

Samuel tapped his slim, tapered fingers together as he scrutinised Damon.

'So my torture wasn't in vain. I'm glad you came to your senses. But I'm still not sure if I'll let you go free. After all, what of your brother?'

Damon smiled chillingly, a look I knew all too well as one he gave before he was going in for a kill. 'I'm sure you can remember from when we were . . . friends,' he said, choking on the word, 'how little fondness I had for Stefan. While he was of assistance recently, I can't say his help has made me like him any better. He's made his choice about how he wants to live, and I'll be damned if he drags me down with him. He's nothing to me,' he said dismissively. 'He's not one of us. Here he is, playing the hidden hero to fallen women of the East End when he could have the world at his feet. I can't associate with a vampire who doesn't embrace his true nature. Even if he was once a brother.'

Samuel nodded once. 'Well, he'll be easy enough to take care of. Tell me more about the girl.'

'I'll do you one better,' Damon said. 'I'll bring you to her tomorrow night. She lives in a two-bit slum with a few other witches, but I'll make sure none of them are around. Come alone. That is, if I have your word that you'll clear my name of these silly charges and stop trying to kill me.'

Samuel's eyes gleamed like two lanterns in the darkness. 'You have my word. I'll exonerate you of all this Jack the Ripper nonsense as soon as the witch is in my possession, alive and well.'

Damon stuck out his hand for him to shake. Samuel grabbed it, and I expected a crash of thunder or a spark to ignite as they shook. But there was nothing except for the whistling of the wind through the bushes.

With a final nod of agreement, Damon turned and walked down the path.

Had that been too easy? I imagined what it would be like if Samuel were able to compel other vampires. The idea filled me with dread. Compulsion, controlling the desires of another soul, was worse than killing. And when creatures already stronger and more lethal than any normal human being were compelled . . . I didn't want to imagine that. It *wouldn't* happen. We'd make sure of it.

Not far away, Hyde Park was lush, empty and prime hunting ground, especially since the Lord Mayor had imposed a curfew on the parks in the wake of the Jack the Ripper murders. That was perfect for me – the wooded areas were free for squirrels, sparrows and hedgehogs to roam.

I stood behind an oak tree, ignoring the rustle of squirrels darting from a leaf pile. I needed something more substantial than a squirrel to quench my thirst. I really needed human blood, but drinking from Lady Alice had made me more determined than ever to avoid it. Her blood had left me feeling more alive and more out of control than I had in years. And I couldn't take that kind of risk right now, especially when Cora and Mary Jane were depending on me.

Drink human blood.

Ever since Cora had said it, I couldn't stop thinking about it. If Cora, a human girl, could imagine – no, *encourage* – me to feed on humans, what was holding me back? It was my true nature. I was a vampire.

A rustle in the bushes caused me to whirl round. It was a woman, laughingly leading a man through the trees. Her sleeve exposed a milky-white shoulder. Their clothing was faded, but clean, and I imagined they were both servants at one of the large houses near the park.

Unbidden, blood rushed to my gums and my fangs elongated. It would be so easy. I wouldn't even have to kill. I could compel. I could approach them saying that I was lost and looking for directions. Then I'd quickly attack, drink and leave.

'Freddy!' The girl grabbed the boy's arm tightly. 'Did you hear something?'

All I heard was the quickening of the girl's blood.

'Just a squirrel, most likely. Besides, I'm here to keep you safe. Give me a kiss?' the man asked.

'Let's go,' the girl said nervously. She guided him by the hand back through the gates, their feet crunching on the autumn leaves.

I could have run after them. I would have enjoyed the hunt, in fact. But that extra step – needing to take that action – stopped me from making a huge mistake. I couldn't bring myself to do it. Couldn't give in to that desire. Not now.

I trained my eyes on the ground, but I was no longer in the mood to hunt. Finally, I grabbed a squirrel from a nearby branch, drained it and threw the carcass to the ground. I kicked a few leaves over it and wished that I had someone to share my hopes and fears with. In a city of a million heartbeats, I was on my own.

CHAPTER 10

'Ready for the big day, brother?' Damon asked as he tweaked at the bow tie around his neck.

I pulled out my pocket watch. Three o'clock.

'Where are you going?' I asked. Damon wasn't supposed to go to Samuel's until six-thirty, and I wasn't due to meet the witches for the praesidium spell until five.

'An errand,' Damon said. 'I'll be back.'

'Don't get arrested again,' I said sulkily. He was still a wanted man.

'Can I come?' Cora piped up from the corner. She'd been quiet ever since the coven meeting.

'Of course.' Damon gave her a crooked smile. 'In fact, I think you should. I intend to spend the afternoon doing some house hunting. Cora, you can help. I think it's important to get a woman's opinion on real estate.'

'You're looking for a *house*?' Was he insane? Did he

realise what we were up against?'

'Yes,' Damon said simply. 'And once I find one, Cora can stay there for the night, then we'll come back and meet her there afterwards. It's the safest thing.'

'How are you going to get a house?' Cora asked.

Damon shrugged. 'Foreclosures, houses up for sale. There are ways for a vampire to live in luxury without having to be invited in.'

'Is that . . . *legal*?'

Damon chuckled. 'In case you haven't noticed, we've been operating outside the law for quite some time, Cora m'dear.'

'I know,' she said quickly. 'I just meant with the vice . . . the vinc . . . the spell between you and Lady Alice. Doesn't that mean no more lying?'

'No lying to *them*. Anyone else is fair game. And besides, I don't think of compelling as lying. It's just strongly suggesting. Witches know it's what we do.'

Cora nodded. 'I just don't want them to be angry with us. They seem scary.'

'Cora, I'm offended!' Damon said in mock horror. 'Do you mean *we're* not as terrifying as we think we are?'

She smiled. 'In your case, your bark is worse than your bite,' she said. 'And I think your brother might be the opposite. I've seen the way he goes after rats.'

It was good-natured teasing, but I felt my shoulders tense all the same. Even Cora recognised that the way I craved blood wasn't normal. I was glad I'd resisted the urge to feed on the humans in Hyde Park.

'Well, as long as Cora's somewhere safe,' I hedged. As if Damon needed my permission to do anything. I hadn't thought of what Cora would do as we carried out our plan. The longer she stayed with us, the less I saw her as a human who needed protecting. As much as I hated to admit it, Damon was right. No matter how tough Cora was, she was still a human, and we needed to make special provisions for her.

'Thanks for your permission, *brother*,' Damon said as he headed to the exit of the tunnel, Cora trailing behind him.

'Remember to bring a stake. And be on time!' I pressed.

I watched my brother retreat as a familiar splinter of doubt lodged its way into my stomach.

Stop it, I said to myself. It was a good idea: Cora needed to hide somewhere safer than Miller's Court or the tunnel. And if Damon wanted a home in London to use after we vanquished Samuel, well, that was his prerogative. I couldn't wait to get out of the city, but Damon never could resist being at the centre of the action.

I scrambled up the ladder into the sunlight, then walked

towards the bridge above the tunnel. A coach was waiting outside a townhouse a few yards down the road. I glanced at a dark horse pawing the cobblestones. As a child, whenever I felt confused, angry or upset, I'd ride my horse, Mezzanotte, into the forest. With each *clip-clop* of her hooves, my thoughts would unwind and my brain would relax. The horse in front of me was nothing like Mezzanotte. It had a patchy black coat and tangled mane.

And yet . . .

I stared into the coachman's watery eyes.

'I need that horse,' I said firmly.

He complacently untied the horse from the carriage. 'All right, gov'nor,' he said, passing me the reins.

I hopped onto its back.

'Hi, girl,' I whispered into her flea-bitten neck. I gently cracked the whip the coachman had given me and took off through the maze of London streets. I wasn't sure where I was going, only that I needed to clear my head.

I ended up riding the horse to Hampstead Heath. From there, I had a view of all London. The city looked beautiful and elegant, with its limestone buildings reaching towards the sky.

I closed my eyes, a vision forming in my mind of a crumbled city, cloudy with smoke, its streets awash with blood and bodies. That's what would happen if Samuel took over. I knew it.

A memory drifted back to me, as sharp and clear as though it had just happened yesterday. My father and I were in the cool, dark woods just beyond our Mystic Falls property. He'd brought Damon and me there to tell us his fear: that the Civil War had awakened vampires, that they could smell blood and that they'd infiltrated the town. Damon got angry at what he'd called my father's 'insane ranting' and stormed off. I had listened.

We are on the side of what is right and good. It is kill or be killed. Do you understand me, boy? This is the war you're being drafted to fight. Right here. It was my father's voice, so distinct and resolute that he could have been standing right next to me.

Twenty years and countless deaths later, the words were still true. I was my father's son, and I knew it was my legacy to save this city from almost certain destruction.

I didn't have any time to waste. Kicking the horse's flank, I rode further into the heath, deep into the brambles. I had hunting to do.

Once I was satiated with the blood of two foxes and three badgers, I jumped back on the horse and made my way to the East End. The sun was rapidly slipping below the horizon, and I already knew I was running late to meet the witches.

I hitched the horse in front of Miller's Court. In an emergency, we could use it for a quick getaway. I knocked on the door. When I didn't hear an answer, I pushed my way in, stake in hand. I'd fashioned it from an oak branch I'd found on the ground at the heath. I liked it. It was elegant, yet powerful. It would do the job. We'd decided it would make the most sense for Damon to have the first opportunity to strike Samuel. After all, he'd be right next to him. But if he failed, I'd be ready.

I stopped short as soon as I walked through the door. Had I entered the wrong house? The stairs had righted themselves, a banister now hung securely along the side and the walls were freshly painted. But the low chanting coming from upstairs assured me that I was in the right place. I hurried up to the second floor and found the witches preparing for the spell.

Lady Alice, clad in a silvery robe, glided down the stairs. 'Stefan, are you ready?'

'I am,' I breathed. Her gardenia-and-jasmine scent assaulted my nostrils, but I didn't feel the same urge to feed as I had two nights before. The only blood I wanted was Samuel's. My father had been right about something else, too: war had awakened the vampire – the angry, destructive force – within me. I was ready for battle.

A blazing fire burned in the circle at the centre of the

room. Next to the fire sat a bench, surrounded by dozens of tall, tapered candles. It looked almost like an altar. On top of it lay Mary Jane, her dark hair loose around her head and topped with a wreath made of intertwined lilac and foxglove. Her friends weren't here, which was for the best. Better for them to be elsewhere, just in case our plan didn't go smoothly.

Lavinia hobbled over to me. She was the only other witch from the coven in attendance, and she wore a silver robe like Lady Alice's. 'Come here, vampire. Sit down,' she said, escorting me to the corner of the room. 'Only witches can take part in this.'

I wordlessly took my seat as the witches crowded closer to Mary Jane, holding hands to form a ring around her. From within them came one low, plaintive note.

The tuneless chant continued until the entire room reverberated. And then the noise abruptly stopped. Lavinia and Lady Alice stepped up to the altar and knelt down, bending their heads so low their foreheads touched the ground.

I glanced around uncomfortably, unsure of whether I too was supposed to bow. But I stayed seated, afraid that even a tiny move would disrupt the energy flowing through the room.

On the bench, Mary Jane's eyes were open, but she didn't

blink. I wondered if she was in a trance as Lavinia opened her mouth and began chanting words rather than sounds.

'*Munimentum, vampiro, eternal . . .*'

The phrase sounded like it was in Latin, a language I'd studied at school, but she was speaking far too quickly for me to understand. As the spell continued, I could see Mary Jane's skin begin to glow as her veins pulsed. I held my breath, trying to send my own Power to the work being done in the middle of the room.

The collection of candles flickered brighter, and the smoke rising from the flames formed a faint blue ring that hovered around the witches.

'*Eterna quite*,' Lavinia said, then clapped three times. The room plunged into darkness as all the candles blew out, as though hit by an enormous gust of wind. And then, just as quickly, the candles relit as if of their own accord. Mary Jane sat up and blinked her eyes.

'Thank you.' She turned to me and smiled. I wasn't sure if it was my imagination, but her skin seemed brighter and her eyes more luminous than ever. But would that be enough protection against Samuel, a monster who seemed to suck light away?

The witches parted, and Mary Jane daintily stepped off the makeshift altar.

'I'm ready,' she said in a clear voice, gazing straight at me.

'Good.' I nodded. 'Now we wait. When Samuel comes, everyone stays here except Mary Jane. If anything should go wrong, Damon will be downstairs to protect her.'

'It won't go wrong. And all Stefan needs to do is kill Seaver. Let us worry about Samuel,' Lavinia said. 'Don't play the hero,' she added, glaring at me sharply.

'I trust Stefan,' Mary Jane said. 'And I trust Alice.' She turned towards Lady Alice and embraced her.

'Thank you,' Lady Alice said, and I could see tears shimmering in her eyes as she pulled away.

'I'll be fine,' Mary Jane assured her. 'I feel strong, ready. That's why I insist no one come downstairs, even if I scream. No one can deviate from the plan.'

'Are you sure?' Lady Alice fretted. 'The praesidium spell can only be used on one member of a coven at a time, so that the recipient is receiving all the energy from the others. But I can perform an *absconditus* spell on myself. It would allow me to hide in plain sight, so I'd be right there with you. You wouldn't be alone.'

'No.' Mary Jane shook her head. 'You've done enough. And I *want* to be alone for this. I'm ready and protected. And Jemima will have all the others in the alley to attack if everything goes awry.'

'It won't,' I said. I turned to follow her down the stairs when Lady Alice pulled me back by the crook of my elbow.

'A word?' she asked.

'Yes?'

'Thank you for saving Mary Jane. I didn't have a chance to say it before. I was too shocked at seeing her after all those years, surrounded by vampires. But I know that you're not the worst.'

Coming from Lady Alice, it was high praise.

'Thank you,' I said, uncomfortably avoiding her gaze. I glanced at the fire, hoping to see an image of the future, but all I could see were dancing orange and red flames. Maybe Lady Alice's magic saw something I didn't. Maybe I *could* be a good man, once Samuel was gone and London was no longer my prison.

The thought filled me with hope as I took my place, crouched at the top of the stairs. Mary Jane stood on the landing below, her eyes closed. She rocked back and forth on her heels and seemed as though she was concentrating deeply.

I closed my eyes briefly as well and tried to muster my Power, hoping I could send it to Mary Jane for strength.

All of a sudden, we heard the whinnying of horses, followed by the ominous thud of one boot, then another, hitting the pavement.

Samuel was here.

Three knocks sounded at the door, followed by Damon's

voice, muffled through the wood.

'Mary Jane!' Damon called. 'Stefan's waiting for you outside.'

This was the agreed code that would cause Mary Jane to open the door. I held my breath as I heard the floorboards creak and the door slowly swing open. Moonlight flooded the landing as Samuel rushed through the door, his eyes gleaming in excitement. Seaver was at his side. At the sight of them Mary Jane gasped, a theatrical effort that impressed me. I leaned forward, my heart surging in my chest. This was going to work.

'Mary Jane. Finally, we meet again.' Samuel leered as he pulled a glittering silver knife from his jacket. I clutched the stake in my hand. I wouldn't jump unless Damon faltered.

As if on cue, Damon pulled a stake from inside his vest.

'So stupid, Samuel,' Damon whispered, a smile crossing his face. But Samuel was faster than Damon had anticipated, and before Damon could stake him, they were caught in a struggle. My breath caught in my throat. I knew what I was supposed to do now: kill Seaver. But with Damon in trouble, my rationale quickly fell by the wayside. I couldn't let Damon die at Samuel's hand.

'You thought you could get the better of me?' Samuel asked, elbowing Damon away. Damon lost his footing and fell to his knees, and I used the opportunity to lurch towards

Samuel, grabbing his neck in a choke hold. The knife fell to the floor, and I hastily pulled out the stake I'd stashed in my boot.

With my arm around his throat, Samuel gasped. I pressed tighter, allowing the point of the stake to graze his chest.

Just then, Seaver rushed through the door and tackled Mary Jane. She tumbled to the ground, screaming, as he held her nose with one hand and pulled a vial from his cloak with the other. She struggled for breath, and at that moment, Seaver forced the liquid down her throat, chanting loudly the whole time.

'Help!' she shrieked.

'Stefan!' I barely heard Lavinia's throaty voice as she clattered through the doorway. It was clear the witches thought the plan was already going awry. But I couldn't focus. Instead, I pressed against the base of the stake. But I didn't have a good angle, and it kept sliding sideways instead of down. I was surprised at how little Samuel was fighting. Did he recognise the futility of the fight? Was he surrendering? *Focus.* I repositioned the stake, ready to drive it into his chest.

'*Asporto!*' Seaver's deep voice yelled, and instantly, I was pushed against the wall as if by an unseen hand. My temple cracked against the wooden wall and blood spurted from my forehead, obstructing my vision. When I went to wipe it away, I found myself unable to lift my arm.

'Help!' I called in a ragged voice, hoping the other witches waiting in the alley would hear. A few feet away, I saw Samuel had got hold of Damon. I closed my eyes, trying to draw my Power up from my centre and push it towards him as Damon wrestled loose from Samuel's grasp. He lunged, but Samuel dodged, and in the process grabbed Mary Jane from where she stood behind Lavinia. Still, I was frozen to the spot, unable to do anything to save Mary Jane.

'*Concisio!*' a female voice yelled. Then I heard a sound like a gunshot, followed by a brilliant white light. It lit up the small room like a firework before once again plunging it into darkness. I turned around. It was Jemima.

'You're free. Kill the witch!' she shrieked. I lunged forward, suddenly unshackled. I plunged the stake into Seaver's back, twisting it until his body fell to the ground. The stake might not have been meant to kill a witch, but it certainly did the trick. At impact, I saw another flash of lightning.

Then I heard Jemima's scream, over and over again. Damon was standing dead still, his eyes locked on Samuel.

'That's right, Damon. Stay where you are like a good boy,' Samuel said smoothly. Blood was dripping from his lips, and his entire body seemed to glow. He tapped his long, tapered fingers together as he surveyed the room. My eyes tracked his gaze and I saw Mary Jane lying crumpled on the ground. My knees buckled under me. There was a crater in the centre of her chest. Her amber eyes were open, her face an unmoving mask of horror. Rivulets of golden liquid were streaming from the hole where her heart should have been. Samuel had done the unimaginable. He'd eaten Mary Jane's heart.

'No!' Lady Alice shrieked, throwing herself on top of Mary Jane's body. I stood, frozen in place, as Damon grabbed the stake from Lavinia's hand and lunged towards Samuel.

'Run!' I pulled Lady Alice from Mary Jane's body. Her robe was smeared with gold-tinged blood as though her heart, too, had been torn out.

'You can't run. Stay still. You too, Stefan,' Samuel said. Damon stopped mid-step, confusion on his face. Samuel had compelled us both. I willed my feet to move, but nothing happened. I was stuck. I felt my stomach and heart clench. The orphans rushed in, too late to the fight, and looked on in horror, although I couldn't tell if they were paralysed by fright or magic.

Samuel laughed. His lips pulled back from his teeth, revealing fangs that glowed gold. 'You see, I got what I came for. And you did, too, even if you're too stupid to realise it. I won't kill you. In trying to betray me, you still fulfilled your end of the bargain. Of course, your good-for-nothing brother killed Seaver, but that's neither here nor there. He was no longer useful to me, so it's just as well. You're free to leave. And I'm feeling magnanimous, so I'll let your brother loose, too. I feel you may have new enemies to keep you busy now,' he said with a demonic laugh.

In the moments since he'd eaten the heart, Samuel had changed. He was taller and stronger, and seemed to be glowing from within. I tried to avoid staring into his eyes, doing anything to resist potential compulsion. Damon blinked, for once at a loss for words.

Samuel kicked Mary Jane's prostrate body and snorted derisively. 'What's one less witch? You should all feel jealous that she died and got to escape this slum. If I were a nice man, I'd give you the same opportunity.' At this, Jemima and the other orphans fled the scene, terrified. I didn't blame them. 'But I have much to do, and none of it includes spending a second longer here than I have to,' he concluded. He picked up Seaver's still-bleeding body and hauled it over his shoulder, walking out and making sure to close the door gently behind him. I heard the whinny of a horse, followed by hoofbeats.

Damon and I locked eyes, and as if by mutual agreement I grabbed the still-keening Lady Alice, and Damon grabbed Lavinia. Together, we made our way to the river. With

139

every footstep, I imagined the agony Mary Jane must have felt in the instant her chest had been ripped open and her heart pulled from her body. I wanted to dive into the inky blackness of the Thames and swim as far as I could, to where the river met the Atlantic and I could swim onward to America.

Finally, when we had put enough distance between us and the house, we stopped. For the moment at least, we were safe. Unlike Mary Jane . . .

I carefully placed Lady Alice on her feet.

'I'm sorry,' I said, knowing the words meant nothing. Anger flashed in her eyes.

'*You* did this,' she spat.

'I tried my best. I killed Seaver. What else could I have done?' I said. My voice was angry, not soothing.

'You could have killed Seaver *before* he removed the spell on Mary Jane. That was your job. But no, you had to go after the glory and try to kill Samuel. That wasn't your place, vampire,' Lavinia said, her voice dripping with hate.

'Calm down. You need to be rational,' Damon said, placing a hand on Lady Alice's shoulder.

'Stop!' she screeched. 'Don't touch me. None of you touch me. You broke your word. Stefan was supposed to follow our plan. He was supposed to kill Seaver. He did it too late and ruined everything. And in doing so, he broke the spell. No more vinculum. We have *nothing* to do with each other now, vampire.'

Lavinia nodded, her eyes hollow. 'Stefan gave his word Mary Jane would be protected. She wasn't. How could you have been so foolish? Only thinking of yourself, and of your brother, when an innocent girl had to pay the price,' she said in disgust. 'Vampires can't be trusted.'

'I'm sorry!' I said again, helplessly. 'But we can't lash out at each other. Don't you see? We have to work together. None of us are safe. Seaver may be dead, but Samuel's still out there, and now that he can compel vampires—'

'Then maybe you'll finally learn how to follow directions. We're done, vampire,' Lady Alice said, her voice cold as ice. Lavinia nodded, glaring at me in silent judgement.

'We've just begun,' I shouted, desperate to get them to realise how vital it was that we work together. 'Don't you see? He can compel anyone now. And that's why we need you more than ever. We need to come up with another spell. Anything to hold him back. And then Damon and I will—'

'Will do what? Nothing. You'll do nothing. I want you both to suffer the way Mary Jane did,' Lady Alice yelled.

'*Deletum vampiro!*' Lavinia intoned, flinging her arms in our direction. As she said the words, the ground beneath us cracked and green weeds began sprouting through the new openings. They quickly grew thicker and taller. Tiny purple flowers sprung from the green stems, and a sickly-sweet smell filled the air. They were vervain plants, larger than I'd ever seen, and they were circling Damon and me, creating a cage. Terror flooded my veins as the scent stung my eyes and made me feel weak. I wanted to collapse, to allow the vervain to overpower me. That was what the witches wanted. It would be so easy to succumb, to finally allow the death I'd escaped for so long to overtake me. Maybe I deserved it.

But not as much as Samuel. The thought tugged against my brain and made me force myself to my knees. Then, I fell back. I was too weak.

'Let's go!' I felt a hand on my arm. Damon.

'I can't!' I protested. The vervain had rendered me nearly unconscious. I felt as though my skin was separating from my body. The only thing I could focus on was the pain penetrating the very core of my being. It was as if I were being burned alive, and I could hear my breathing, wet and ragged, below the sound of Lavinia's demonic laughter.

'Get up!' Damon commanded as he dragged me to my feet and pulled me past the vervain plants. The pain intensified to a place beyond agony. I felt my body being hoisted on top of Damon's shoulders as he broke into a run.

My eyelids fluttered closed. My mind wandered back to Mystic Falls on a moonless night.

I was frantically riding Mezzanotte through the forest, an unconscious and transitioning Damon splayed over the saddle. Jonathan Gilbert and the other townspeople were in pursuit close behind us. Mezzanotte galloped, jumping over felled trees and sidestepping branches. But she was wounded by their bullets, and foam spewed from her mouth. The townspeople's anger spurred their adrenalin, and they were gaining on us. I drove my heel into Mezzanotte's flank as another fallen tree blocked our path. She gracefully leaped over the trunk, but then collapsed.

'No!' I protested. I didn't want Mezzanotte to die. I shifted and fell to the ground with a thud, alongside my dead horse . . .

I opened my eyes and found myself staring up at the inky black London sky. I looked down and saw raised vervain welts on my hands and arms.

'Finally. You're awake,' Damon said disgustedly, but I could see the relief in his face.

I blinked. We were on the lawn of a well-kept house in a quiet square. The house was red brick and three storeys tall, set back from the road and ringed by a black iron fence. Several large oak trees filled the small front yard, giving the house even more privacy.

'Where are we?' The large trees brought to mind the graceful houses on the outskirts of New Orleans, while the three-storey townhouse reminded me of the ones in New

York. How long had we been running? I wondered if maybe we weren't in London at all, and that somehow, everything had been a horrible dream.

'Bedford Square,' Damon said dismissively. 'It's rather small. The Earl of Erne lived there, until the latest scandal stripped him of his title and home. He won't be back for a while.'

I nodded. I knew he wanted me to be impressed by his acquisition, but I couldn't stop thinking about Samuel and Mary Jane.

'It's over,' I said slowly, the events coming back to me in hideous clarity. Mary Jane's heart. Samuel's triumph. Lavinia's spell and Lady Alice's sorrow. 'Either the witches will kill us, or Samuel will.'

'No. Samuel won a battle. He didn't win the war. And this is war, brother.'

'So what are we going to do?' I asked.

'Whatever it takes,' Damon said. Angry red burn marks from the vervain crisscrossed his hands and face. I looked at my own skin. Compared to my mental anguish, these wounds were the equivalent of mosquito bites.

'Whatever it takes,' I repeated. I pushed my bruised, battered body to my feet and followed Damon to the door of the house. But I knew no change in location would make a damn bit of difference.

CHAPTER 11

Damon opened the door and I staggered into the house in Bedford Square. It was warm, dark and quiet. I found a small guest room; the bed was made up with a thick wool blanket and I fell into it gladly.

I woke to the sun streaming through the window. Despite the cheerful surroundings, my stomach plummeted as I remembered the terrible night. But I gathered my courage. Somehow, we would find a way to defeat Samuel and avenge Mary Jane's death. We had to.

I quickly went to the closet and pulled out a starched shirt and a pair of trousers. For a stranger's clothing, they fitted fairly well. I made my way down a curving oak staircase to the downstairs parlour. The house may have been small for Damon's taste, but it was elegantly decorated with antique cherrywood furniture and intricately woven oriental carpets. The walls were covered with ornate patterned wallpaper and gilt mirrors, and delicate crystal chandeliers hung from the ceilings. I'd frequently found myself in abandoned houses before – no matter where in the world we were, Lexi had a knack for discovering dilapidated houses and making them home – but this was in pristine condition. Damon had done well.

Downstairs, Cora was relaxing in a wingback chair. She was wearing a green velvet dress far too large for her tiny frame. Her copper hair was lustrous and she looked alert, but the dark shadows under her eyes betrayed her anxiety. Damon must have told her what had happened with Samuel. A newspaper was open in her lap, but her eyes were darting frantically across the page, and I could tell she wasn't reading so much as desperately scanning for anything about what had happened in the East End the night before.

'Look at this,' Cora said flatly, not bothering to say hello. She pointed to an article.

'Did you go outside by yourself to get that?' I asked hoarsely.

She didn't answer, but pointed her finger at the article.

JACK THE RIPPER KILLS AGAIN!

I continued reading. Mary Jane's discarded body had been found by a rent collector in the Miller's Court flat. Of course, neither Samuel nor the witches were mentioned. I continued to read.

Dr Thomas Bond and Dr George Phillips examined the body, and discovered that unlike the other Ripper victims, this one was missing a heart. An inquest is being held in Shoreditch. Anyone who was in the vicinity of Miller's Court the night of 8th November is urged to go to the police immediately with any information.

'This doesn't say anything we don't already know,' I said, pushing the paper away.

'Keep reading,' Cora said, pointing to a paragraph a third of the way down the page. I skimmed the text.

Sources are confident the killings were not the work of previous suspect Damon de Sangue. Scotland Yard is now narrowing its focus on the Duke of Clarence, seen near several crime scenes and currently presumed missing. If anyone sees the Duke, or has any intelligence as to the Ripper's identity, they are to speak immediately to either Scotland Yard or the Metropolitan Police.

'At least Damon's free now. But Samuel has Mary Jane's heart,' Cora said in a small voice. 'How could the life of someone as innocent as Mary Jane lead to harm? It doesn't make sense.'

'I know.' I thought of the brave way Mary Jane had faced

Samuel. I thought of how she so easily befriended Damon and me, despite the fact that vampires and witches were supposed to be mortal enemies.

Maybe her stubbornness had been the weak spot that had killed her. She was one more victim to add to the far-too-long list of people whose deaths I'd been responsible for.

'It was my fault,' I said finally. 'I should have thought of what could have gone wrong. I should have killed Seaver first. If I'd just stuck with the plan, Samuel would have been trapped.' I sighed heavily.

'Stop it!' Cora snapped. 'Do you know how often you blame yourself? Damon was in trouble, and he needed your help. It's not your fault, and the more you say it, the more you'll believe it. The more *I'll* believe it. Just . . . stop. All right?'

'All right,' I echoed. But deep down, I knew I'd done it because I'd wanted to kill Samuel. I'd wanted to feel my stake puncturing his chest. But I didn't explain that to Cora. I couldn't bear to see disappointment in her eyes.

Luckily, just then Damon walked down the curved staircase, wearing a blue smoking jacket trimmed with white fur. 'What's all the racket?'

'The Ripper made the papers again,' I said dryly, smoothing the broadsheet and passing it to him.

He perched on the end of the low-slung cherrywood

chair in the corner. Soon, a smile spread across his face as he shoved the paper aside.

'Well, it looks like I'll be able to reintroduce myself to society. It'll be nice to be free after being a wanted man for so long. I'm ready to resume my life of luxury.'

I stared at my brother. Could he possibly be serious? "What about Samuel?' I asked.

'What about Samuel?' Damon echoed, perfectly mocking my inflection. 'You know, brother, I was thinking last night that maybe you've been right all along. Maybe we should leave the country with our tails between our legs. We had a plan. We had Power. We had witches. And we had numbers on our side. And yet Samuel and his Asylum goon overtook us.'

'You could have warned us he was bringing reinforcements.'

'I didn't know. Seaver must have been tailing us. And why did it matter? You were supposed to kill him if he came. I saw you when I was fighting with Samuel. You were right behind him. You could have stabbed him in the back, *then* tried to help me. Ever think of that, brother?'

'Shut up!' Cora yelled as she shot to her feet and angrily placed her hands on her hips. 'I won't listen to you two bicker! If this continues, I'll leave,' she said, her eyes flashing.

Damon and I reflexively looked at her, then at each other. If Cora left, we'd be alone together. And that wouldn't work. She was like a mediator: we needed her presence for us to work effectively. If she wasn't there, either we'd argue our way to inaction, or our alliance would self-destruct.

'Don't leave,' I said to Cora. 'But I think we can all agree we need a new perspective on the situation. We all want to kill Samuel. But we don't know how to do it. I think we should talk to James and see what he thinks. We can't do this alone.'

'And what if James decides he's done with vampires and stakes you? I've known him a long time. He's fickle,' Damon countered.

'I'm willing to take the risk,' I said quietly.

'Are you?' he asked. 'You know what your problem is? You think too much. You don't act, and that's dangerous. And until you stop torturing yourself with your conscience, we can't work together.'

'I don't think you can blame me for thinking too much based on what happened last night. And that's why I need to see James. To find out how strong Samuel really is. Maybe James will know of a weakness in his new powers.'

'Whatever you say. I'm too hungry to fight. Go do your detective work. I'll be breakfasting at Bailey's Hotel. I can't possibly think until I've had a good meal.'

I blanched, knowing that Damon's idea of a good meal meant an attractive woman. 'Fine.'

It was the same old story: when Damon was near death, he was my brother, the man I'd do anything for – including risking my own life. But when he was well, his barrage of caustic comments chipped away at my goodwill.

As soon as he left, Cora turned to face me. A small smile played on her lips.

'What?' I asked, ready for another round of insults.

'Nothing really.' She shook her head. 'It's just that together, you and Damon complete each other. You think, and he's all about action. But instead of appreciating what the other has, you fight about it.'

I nodded but didn't say anything. I didn't want to talk about our brotherly relationship. I wanted to figure out if there was any way to stop Samuel. But I was worried it was impossible. Not without a force greater than ourselves.

'Let's see James,' I said gruffly.

Cora nodded, and together we walked out of the house and made our way to James's emporium. The sun was shining brightly, and the cold snap had receded. In fact, men were walking the streets with their jackets over their arms, and people were sunning themselves on the steps of Trafalgar Square. Still, everywhere we walked, we heard snatches of conversation:

'Killed in her bed . . .'

'Heart torn out as if she were attacked by an animal . . .'

'I'm telling you, no one is safe.'

'What's America like?' Cora asked quietly as we zigzagged our way through the crowded pavements of Fleet Street.

'Big,' I said, knowing that she was mostly asking to distract me from the chatter around us. 'You'd like it.' I thought of Cora, stepping off a steamer boat and into a world where she wouldn't be assaulted on a daily basis by memories of Violet. I thought of the Irish neighborhoods that had sprung up in Boston and New York and San Francisco. She'd definitely find a home.

Maybe Cora should go to America. At least that way, I wouldn't have to worry about her being next on the list of my accidental victims. 'Do you want to go?' I asked gently.

She sighed. 'I don't know. If I left, I'd never see my family again. They don't even know Violet's dead. I've been trying to decide if I should tell them or let them think that she just got . . . too busy to write.'

'Would they believe that?' I asked sceptically.

Cora smiled wanly. 'They would. They always said that London would change us. They'd think that if we were happy, then they'd done their job. I think they'd rather imagine Violet had become a snob, not wanting to introduce her parents to her posh new friends, than find out she was dead. They'd never believe she'd been turned into a vampire and killed by her own sister. I don't even believe that,' she said sadly.

'They only wanted you to be happy?' I asked, thinking back to my own father. At this point, he'd been dead for longer than Cora had been alive, and yet no matter how far I was from his grave or how many years passed, I couldn't escape his voice. *Salvatore men fight, even if it's to the death.* After all, that's what he'd done. He'd shot me, his own son.

'Yes,' Cora sighed. 'They wouldn't be able to live if they knew what happened to Violet. They would blame themselves for letting her go. And then if they knew I wasn't there to take care of her . . . that I was the one who killed her . . .'

I gently rested my hand on her arm. 'Look at me,' I said, stopping in the street as pedestrians streamed around us. I gazed into her deep-blue eyes. 'You haven't done anything wrong. And what happened to that speech about not blaming yourself? If none of the events are my fault, then they're definitely not yours. Is that a deal?'

The corners of her lips twisted, but she didn't smile. 'I know. It's just hard.'

I nodded. There were no words of wisdom I could give her, nor were there any to console her. *We're in it together? At least you have me?* I was sure being reminded she was bound to a vampire would offer little comfort.

Soon, we reached the emporium. I rang the doorbell and stepped back. For the first time, I noticed that the door was decorated with a chain of blue flowers. It was clearly a charm, but against what?

James opened the door and looked up at us from his height of only three feet.

'Hello,' I said, glancing down and noticing that a few red boils had popped, blooming like roses on his pockmarked skin. As always, his one eye was red and watery, while the place where his other eye should have been was a cavernous, empty socket.

'You're still alive, vampire. And you've managed to get your girl back. Impressive,' James said as he hustled us into the shop. 'So sit down. Have some tea. Tell me what you've been doing.' Without looking at me, James began fussing at the tiny stove in the corner of the room. I glanced around the shelves crammed full of jars of eyeballs, beating hearts and two-headed mice. There *had* to be something here to protect us from Samuel.

'We need to talk to you about last night,' Cora said smoothly, causing James to turn from the stove, a tin mug in each hand.

'Earl Grey for you both. What do you mean, "last night"?' he asked, squinting his one eye at Cora. He shuffled towards us, upsetting a fat cat that was lazing in his path. The cat hissed and darted under the table, where it flicked its tail back and forth against my ankle.

'Samuel attacked again. And this time, he did more than kill,' Cora said.

At this, James slammed the two metal mugs down on the table so forcefully that the wooden table legs began to buckle.

'Damn it!' he said. He grabbed a jar full of dead turtles from a nearby shelf, pulled one out and placed it under an uneven table leg to keep it steady. 'Quit speaking in riddles, girl! Do I look like that fool Ephraim? Now, tell the whole story, and start from the beginning.'

'Yes, sir!' Cora gulped. 'Stefan and Damon met a girl, Mary Jane, who turned out to be a purebred witch. And they realised that Samuel wanted her heart. So—'

'We allied ourselves with a coven using the vinculum spell,' I cut in. 'After that was in place, they used praesidium on Mary Jane. We thought that we'd use her to lure Samuel, then trap him and kill him. But he brought along a witch who had a potion that reversed the spell. He outsmarted us,' I explained.

'And he ate the heart?' James asked, his face, even the reddish boils, draining of colour. He closed his eyes and shook his head.

'Yes,' Cora and I said in unison.

He sighed and sat down heavily. 'This is bad,' he said. 'This is very, very bad.'

'I know,' I said. 'That's why we came to you. We need help.'

'Of course you need help! But the problem is, I can't give it to you. Your whole story is the perfect example of why vampires are bad for my business and bad for society. They always think they can control the world. They think no one else matters but them. But they don't understand what they're doing in the process!' he fumed, standing and overturning his chair in his fury. He pulled down the blinds and bolted the door before crossing to the bookcase and hauling books off the shelves. Finally, he found what he was looking for: a thin, threadbare, red volume. He frantically turned the pages with his chubby hands as Cora and I glanced at each other. I was afraid to even breathe.

'Listen to this story, vampire,' James muttered. 'Then you'll know what you're dealing with.' The cat hissed, and I felt all the eyeballs in the jar on the shelf staring at me.

James gulped Cora's untouched tea and wiped his mouth with the back of his hand before he flipped one more page. He glanced at it and nodded, as if the words proved some unspoken point. 'There's a town in the middle of Prussia called Tulpedorf,' he said, tripping over the foreign pronunciation. 'Or rather, there was a town. It doesn't exist any more,' he continued evenly, the colour beginning to return to his face.

'What happened?' Cora asked, leaning forward.

'A vampire moved in,' James explained. 'Kind of like your Samuel – a man with a terrible mission. Elijah was his name. No one knew where he came from, or who he was. He was a stranger, but remarkably charismatic. People liked him, and there was even some whispering that he should rule the town. The more people whispered that, the more people started to believe it. After all, strange things were happening around town. Animal attacks, mysterious deaths. Maybe Elijah would save them. Little did they know, he was a vampire. One day, he did take over the town. He rounded up an army of the villagers he'd been turning into vampires ever since he arrived and compelled them to do his bidding. They stormed the castle of the local lord. Then, of course, his army began killing innocent citizens. For two days, there was mass carnage. But just as quickly as it began, it stopped. Elijah called off his vampire army. He compelled them to head to the woods and find as many branches as they could. Once there was an enormous pile of kindling, Elijah lit a match and ordered the army to step into the flames. They did, without a second thought. At this point, everyone in the town who had survived the massacre just watched in horror.

Some screamed for them to stop. But no one did. Elijah did it just because he could, you see? He played with people, like a puppeteer, and didn't care about the consequences. And that was a tiny town. One can only imagine what a man with ambition and numbers would do in a city like London.'

'Where did Elijah go?' I asked.

'No one knows.' James shrugged. 'But that's neither here nor there. I'm telling you this story so you know exactly what your Samuel is now capable of. But something tells me he won't be content with a few dozen murders.'

'So what do we do?' Cora asked. 'Is there some sort of antidote? I know vervain stops humans from falling under compulsion. If we could just find another herb that would protect vampires, then we could fill the water supply or . . .' She trailed off.

'There is no herb,' James said. 'Vervain won't work against his power. It might protect humans against any of the vampires Samuel will compel, but how long do you think that will last? Any job that can't be carried out by one of his minions, I'm sure Samuel will simply perform himself. I can't help you. And I can't have either of you coming to my shop any more. It's too dangerous. I'm leaving here myself.'

'I understand,' I said heavily, glancing futilely at the shelves.

'Come on, vampire,' he said, unbolting the door. Cora

and I stood on the threshold as James hurriedly began plucking jars and boxes off the shelves and placing them on the table. He opened a small bottle filled with green liquid and gulped it down, then turned round when he realised I was still staring at him.

'Go!' James yelled. Cora and I fled. At the far end of the alley, I looked back. James was standing outside the shop, throwing stems of vervain over the welcome mat. Even the shop catering to monsters wouldn't have me any more.

CHAPTER 12

I felt like I was the bumbling villain in a burlesque show. Despite being foiled time and time again, I insisted on trying a new scheme. But in a burlesque show, there was an audience. And I couldn't help but wonder: was Samuel watching? I hoped he was, if nothing else than as a distraction from building his vampire army.

When Father had planned a siege against the vampires in our town, he'd done it methodically, making sure everyone knew what their roles were: Jonathan Gilbert was supposed to find vampires with his compass, Honoraria Falls was supposed to distribute vervain to everyone, and Sheriff Forbes was to supply the brute manpower, muzzles and chains to hold the vampires until their destruction. How much easier would a siege be if the commander could compel everyone – even his enemies – to do his bidding with a simple thought?

We were out of options, but as foolish as it might have been, I couldn't stop trying to save the city. I was the only one who could.

As I desperately racked my brain for another idea, I couldn't help but feel like the curtains were about to fall on the show. The only question was: how would it end?

In the short time we'd been in James's shop, the weather had changed completely. The sun had disappeared behind a cloud, the air was cold and sharp and the ground was coated in a fine layer of white snow. Cora, chilled to the bone, headed back to Bedford Square, while I continued to walk. The flurries had the effect of making London look like an etching on a Christmas card. The air was redolent with the scent of roasted chestnuts, and rosy-cheeked people were marvelling at the accumulation of snow on the pavement. Men stopped on the streets to jovially slap one another on the backs in greeting. All around me London seemed at its finest, while all I felt was grief and despair.

Everyone had turned on us. Including the witches. But I knew, deep down, that Lady Alice would want to avenge Mary Jane's death as much as I did. The image of the terrible gold-tinged blood frothing at Samuel's mouth sprung to my mind. I wouldn't let Mary Jane's death fuel evil. And if Lady Alice loved her as much as she said, she wouldn't either. Making up my mind, I headed to Lady Alice's house. Was it a suicide mission? Maybe. I knew she hated me. But she was also our only hope.

By the time I reached the mansion, my boots were soaked and my fingers felt raw from the cold. I tentatively pushed the iron gate, surprised when it swung open without force. She must not have sensed my presence, because walking down the path was Lady Alice herself, wearing a shapeless white robe that looked like a burial shroud.

'Stefan,' she said briefly. I could tell that behind her back she gripped a stake. She was ready for anything.

Silence hung in the air as we appraised each other. I knew she might attack at any second, and I felt my heart hammering in my chest. I wondered if she could hear it.

I imagined the stake coming towards my chest. I'd dodge, before trying to knock it out of her hand. I'd want to reason with her. But unbidden, another more terrifying image sprang to my mind. The wooden point would graze my chest and my fangs would appear. In an instant, I'd sink my teeth into Lady Alice's neck and tear her throat out, stopping only when her body was drained. I mashed my lips together and avoided her gaze. When I was provoked, I was no longer Stefan. I was a monster.

'I'm not here to fight,' I said, profoundly hoping it was the truth. 'I just want to talk. I'll agree to whatever terms make you feel comfortable.'

Lady Alice hesitated, and I could see that she was weighing her options.

'All right.' She nodded. 'I'll give you a few minutes. Come with me.' She gestured for me to follow her down the winding walkway and to a gravel pathway behind the house. In its centre was a single rose bush, bursting with red blossoms despite the weather. I followed her, matching her slow, careful steps.

'As good as gold,' she murmured as she neared the centre. Once there, she turned to face me. The setting sun illuminated her face. 'It's funny – people say that all the time without really knowing what it means. But in Mary Jane's case, I saw it with my own eyes. She truly was as good as gold. And now that good has been turned evil. You broke vinculum, and I do blame you for what has happened. But I won't kill you. Still, here's what you need to know, Stefan,' she said in a low voice, her eyes blazing. 'I know you'll ask me to help you, and I know you'll say that you're not asking for yourself. You'll say that you're asking for the greater good, and that London is in grave danger.'

'Yes,' I began, nodding. 'But—'

'I know you're going to say that you're doing this for Mary Jane. That if we don't do something, her life was in vain.'

'Y-y-yes,' I said hesitantly.

'But I can't help you,' she said finally. 'I'm not like you. I

163

can't just drink blood and be good as new. I need time to grieve. And I can't work with people I don't trust. Because you betrayed me, Stefan. You may not have meant to, but you gave me your word, and your word was false. Words have power. And when that power is undermined . . .' She shook her head. 'I suppose it's like when one of your kind gets staked. Not in the heart, so it doesn't kill you. But it drains your Power.'

'I understand,' I said. 'But this isn't just about us. Now that Samuel has the power to compel vampires, he can control the whole city. Innocent lives will be lost. I won't ask you to fight, but can't you help us? Could you make more eleuthro?'

She sighed heavily. 'No, Stefan. I can't make eleuthro.' She reached towards the rose bush, touching one of the flowers. The petals fell to the earth like drops of blood on the thin white layer of snow. 'Witches only have as much power as their coven. And right now, we're all in mourning, all unsure how we'll handle this . . . *situation*. We will band together again if we find one of our own in danger, but we will not help the likes of you. That much is certain. And until I have the support of my coven, I don't have any power at all.'

'I'm sorry,' I said again.

'Sorry doesn't bring back Mary Jane. Now go. You've said enough. I can't bear to hear any more.'

I nodded mutely and turned my back, shuffling down the pathway.

'Hello, brother,' Damon said, startling me by bursting into my bedroom. He was wearing a suit with a black silk ascot tied round his neck. He dropped a similarly expensive-looking suit on the foot of my bed. It was later that evening, and I'd spent the last hour frowning into my notebook, desperately trying to come up with a plan. But I couldn't. I could barely even write. *Words have power*, Lady Alice had said. Well, the blank page in front of me certainly didn't. I was out of ideas.

But while I was miserable, Damon seemed positively overjoyed. He held a crystal glass in his hands. 'Would you like a drink?'

I shook my head. 'I have nothing to celebrate.'

'Who said you need a reason to celebrate?' He pushed the glass closer to me.

'You want to celebrate while Samuel's probably rounding up a vampire army?' I concentrated on the dimly glowing lapis lazuli stone set in the ring on my finger so I could avoid his gaze. 'I'm not in the mood.'

'Why? Because a witch yelled at you?' Damon asked pointedly. He sat in a chair in the corner and swirled his glass. 'Cora told me you saw Lady Alice, and it didn't go well.

What did you expect? A hero's welcome and a six-course dinner? We tried to use magic, and it didn't work. So now we go to Plan D,' he said, downing his glass and holding it out to me in a mock toast.

'Plan drunk?' I asked wryly.

'That's a good one!' he said enthusiastically. 'But no. Plan *Damon*.'

'And what would that be?' I asked, turning to face him. 'Is that "Kill all of London before Samuel does it first"? Is it "Compel your way into millions of pounds before running away"? Or is it "Go over to his side, because you always want to be the one to win"?'

'None of the above.' Damon shrugged. 'But I will say it's far better than moping, which is Plan Stefan.'

I glanced back at my notebook so he wouldn't see the redness rise to my cheeks. Was that true? And why did I care? Damon liked to deliberately provoke, and no matter what, I walked into his trap.

Just then I heard a light knock on the door.

'Come in!' I called, grateful for the interruption.

Cora entered the room, the train of a red silk dress trailing on the floor behind her.

'Stefan, are you feeling better?' she said.

'I'm fine, I just had a headache. I still do,' I said.

'Well, I would too if I spent all my time moping,' Damon

said. 'Come on! I still haven't told you my plan. My name has been cleared, we're not dressed like paupers and I think the only thing we can do is go out tonight. There are dozens of balls in honour of the Lord Mayor's Parade. Why, there's even one at White's that Lord Ainsley is giving. I heard about it this morning at breakfast.'

'That isn't a plan, it's a party. You can go if you want, but I'm going to stay here and think.'

'It's a *party* with people who know Samuel. We go, we gather information, and then we plan. Who knows? Maybe we can even prevent some attacks. It's worth a try.'

Cora nodded. 'That sounds like a good idea. After all, if we're there, maybe we can find out if Samuel's already starting to turn people into vampires. And maybe we'll find information about what he's doing with them.'

I glanced from Cora to Damon. Both were staring at me, willing me to say yes. What did I have to lose? The childish part of me wanted to stay in, but I realised they were right. At this point, the only thing we could do was gather as much information as possible.

'All right. I'll be down in a moment,' I said.

Ten minutes later, courtesy of a compelled coach driver, we were in front of what looked like an average residence in central London. It was a townhouse, with a lit gas lamp at the front. The only sign that it was a nightclub was the stream of people constantly entering and exiting. To the left of the entrance, a man in a top hat sat on a high stool, scrutinising a list of names.

'Welcome to White's!' Damon said grandly, as if it were his own private establishment. I rolled my eyes as I helped Cora out of the carriage.

On hearing Damon's voice, the man by the door looked up.

'Count de Sangue. Welcome back!' He bowed with a flourish and ushered us inside. We walked down a carpeted staircase and into the party.

'Just like old times.' Damon sighed happily, rubbing his hands together. The air was filled with the sound of instruments tuning up, ice cubes clinking in highball glasses and chattering conversations punctuated by laughter. The crush of the crowd created an intoxicating aroma, and every thought in my brain was superseded by the sound of hundreds of heartbeats *th-thumping* under the din.

'Why, hello there!' A girl's voice yanked me from my reverie. I whirled round to see a tall woman with dainty features and butterscotch-coloured hair. I sniffed, taking in the burned-coffee smell of her blood. Her slow, sleepy smile and slight waver indicated it would almost certainly be tinged with rum, and I could imagine my fangs gently sliding against her skin until . . .

'Charlotte!' Damon said, licking his upper lip. 'You have no idea how much I've missed you.'

Charlotte. I stepped back as though I'd been slapped. I'd been so entranced by the scent of her blood that I'd forgotten I knew her. She was the actress Damon had taken up with before the Jack the Ripper accusations. I hastily took a glass of wine from a passing waiter's tray, downing it fast. Hopefully the alcohol would numb my craving for blood.

'Well, I can't say the same of you, you brute,' Charlotte said. She pouted, but I could tell from the way her eyes danced that she was only putting on a display of anger. 'Not only did you *disappear*, but you became a wanted criminal in the blink of an eye. Of course, I knew it wasn't true. You only travel in the best circles, so you'd never go to that awful East End, even if you were a murderer.' She laughed. Her fingers grazed her neck. It was an unconscious gesture, but seeing it caused my pulse to pound.

'It really is rather funny, when you think about it. Me, in the East End, with prostitutes, when I could be here, with you on my arm.' Damon flashed her one of his charming half-smiles.

'It is, isn't it?' Charlotte laughed again, but her eyes seemed hollow. Something about her was amiss, but I couldn't put my finger on it. I hadn't known her well, but on the few occasions our paths had crossed, she'd always seemed flirtatious. Now her statements were half a second too slow, as if she were struggling to remember her lines. She ran her finger along Damon's collarbone. 'Well, you'll have to tell us all about life on the lam. How delightfully slum-worthy it must have been.'

'Oh, believe me, it was,' he said. 'But more important, tell me about you. What have I missed?'

This was Damon's plan for the evening? To flirt his way back into society?

But Charlotte smiled, oblivious of me and my frustration as she turned all her womanly charms on Damon. 'Well, I just opened a new play. It's called *The Temptress*, and you can only imagine what my part is,' she said suggestively, arching a blonde eyebrow.

'Perfect casting,' Damon said, smoothly taking her hand in his. But before he could kiss it, she snatched it away.

'You'll have to get me a drink first,' she demanded. 'You have a lot of apologising to do for disappearing on me like that.'

'I'm at your service,' he said, wiggling his eyebrows.

I turned away, disgusted, even though I shouldn't have been surprised. Damon's reaction to death and destruction was always to dance through the ashes. Instead of dwelling on it, I took in my surroundings. In the centre of the room, the band struck up one of the current music hall favourites.

I stopped when I saw the curving staircase that led up to the hotel. Ordinarily, white-gloved staff would be guarding the stairs to ensure partygoers without hotel keys didn't slip past. Tonight, however, there were none. In fact, despite the bustling atmosphere, the evening seemed odd. Dancers were half a step behind the music, conversations sounded stilted and hardly anyone had touched the sumptuous buffet table, laden with éclairs, oysters from the Atlantic, and cheeses and meats from France. But although there wasn't anything on the buffet table I wanted, it was strange that the other partygoers felt the same. Could they all be thirsting for blood?

I heard a sound coming from the upper landing. It could have merely been a porter moving a piece of furniture, or two lovers who'd found a quieter spot to entertain each other. But I decided to investigate. After all, if my suspicions were correct, someone might be in trouble.

I stole quietly up the staircase. When I reached the landing, it was just what I'd feared. One of the well-dressed men from downstairs was holding a servant girl in an embrace. But the girl wasn't reciprocating. Instead, she'd fallen over his arms in a faint, and he was sucking blood from her neck.

Before I knew what I was doing, I raced towards them. I

didn't have vervain or a stake. But I had Power. I hoped that would be enough.

The vampire turned to me, his eyes blazing in surprise as he dropped the girl to the ground. I could tell he was a brand-new vampire. His feeding had been manic and forceful, his chin at an awkward angle to her throat.

I bared my fangs and emitted a low, guttural growl that sent the vampire beating a hasty retreat. As he vanished down the staircase, the servant girl sat up, rubbing her head.

'What happened?' she asked in confusion, unaware of the two small wounds still dripping blood down her neck.

'You passed out. You must have been exhausted.' I compelled her to believe it. 'You should head home.'

I felt the lining of my pocket, surprised when my fingertips grazed several heavy coins. The owner of this pair of trousers was obviously wealthy. I pulled the coins out.

'Here,' I said, dropping the change into the girl's hand. 'This should pay you for tonight.'

She smiled a slow, sleepy smile. 'Thank you, sir. I feel like you're my guardian angel.'

'Trust me, I'm not,' I said roughly.

I escorted her down the stairs, making sure she left the building safely. Then I turned to survey the scene. I had to find the vampire before he did more damage.

My heart dropped. How had I not noticed before? Even

though Samuel wasn't here, he was everywhere: stamped on the blank faces of the men eschewing the buffet table, in the hollow gestures of women adjusting their neck scarves and in the sombre, funereal atmosphere. It wasn't as if the partygoers were doing anything unusual or out of place. Rather, their movements were studied and deliberate, as if they were performing on a stage. Mostly, it was their vacant stares that made it obvious.

They were all vampires. And they were all compelled.

I saw Cora weave her way through the crowd towards me. At least she was safe. 'Stefan, where *were* you?' she asked, placing her hands on her hips. 'I've been looking for you. Lord Ainsley's right over there.'

Ahead of us was a ginger-haired man I'd met several times, back when Damon was part of Samuel's elite social circle. He was heir to a British banking fortune and had always seemed to be one of Samuel's closest confidants.

'Lord Ainsley!' I called loudly. I needed to see for myself if he was compelled, too. A few people, including Cora, turned to stare. Lord Ainsley nodded briefly, ended his conversation and began picking his way towards me. He was only a few feet away when a short man in a tailcoat, top hat and bow tie lurched in front of me. I held out my arm to keep him from falling. As I steadied him, his glazed eyes turned up towards me and he blinked in confusion.

'Are you all right?' I asked in annoyance.

He nodded, then his eyes narrowed suspiciously. 'Do I know you?'

'Friend of Samuel's,' I lied as Cora squeezed my hand. 'Is he coming tonight?'

The man shook his head. 'We know how busy Samuel is. He's got business at Ten Downing Street. Say, will you be going tomorrow? I hear he's only picking a few of his best soldiers to join him.'

'Downing Street?' The name sounded familiar, but I couldn't place it. There was no response; the man had already faded back into the crowd.

At this point, we'd lost Lord Ainsley, too. I saw Damon, twirling Charlotte in the centre of the dance floor, as though nothing was wrong. Her movements were wooden.

I had to get Cora out of there before she became the party's next victim. I grabbed her arm and began weaving between the dancers towards Damon.

I tapped his shoulder. 'A word?'

He glanced at me, annoyance evident in his face. 'Yes, brother?'

'In *private*,' I said.

'You can go ahead,' Charlotte said stiffly.

Not taking my hand off Cora's arm, I led the way outside, away from any prying eyes. My breath came out in white puffs in the cold.

I locked eyes with my brother. 'Do you know what's going on in there?' I asked.

'That the party's full of vampires? Yes, and apparently, compelled vampires are as dull as dishwater,' he said disdainfully.

'We have to leave, Damon. It's not safe here.'

He shrugged. 'Relax. I'll have a few more dances, then maybe a quick meal off a servant girl. I'll be right behind you.'

'Fine, do what you like,' I said in disgust. 'I'll see you at home.' Let Damon shirk responsibility in favour of one last dance. I was determined to prevent anyone else from falling into the clutches of Samuel's army of vampires.

Without another word, I hailed one of the cabs waiting on the corner and directed it back to our Bedford Square home.

CHAPTER 13

'What happened?' Cora asked when we finally made our way back to the house. 'That wasn't a normal party. Samuel's already hard at work,' I said, explaining what I'd seen upstairs. 'His next stop is Ten Downing Street.' Cora's face whitened, and then she turned on her heel and marched into the kitchen.

'What are you doing?' I called, trailing behind her as she flung open the cupboards and pulled out bags of flour and sugar before placing them on the rough-hewn wooden table in the centre of the room.

'If we want to have any chance of getting in to stop Samuel, we'll need reinforcements. You do know what Ten Downing Street is, don't you?'

I shook my head.

'It's where Robert Cecil lives. The prime minister?' Cora said in exasperation. 'Stefan, this is serious!'

'I know it is. If he gets inside, then he can turn him and compel him to do his bidding.' I hung my head in my hands. 'But how, exactly, will baking help solve this problem?' I asked as I watched Cora pour flour onto a scale. A smudge of it landed on her cheek, but she didn't bother to wipe it off.

'Vervain,' she said crisply. 'We'll bribe the guards with vervain-laced biscuits, so they'll be protected from compulsion when Samuel arrives. I think Damon still has some lying around. I saw it in his bag upstairs. It's in a vial – be a dear and get it?' she asked sweetly.

I happily obliged, glad someone was able to come up with a plan. Sure enough, Damon had several vials of vervain, along with a crossbow and wooden bullets. He was well stocked for a vampire battle. *He should have brought that to the party*, I thought darkly as I gingerly grabbed the vervain bottles and brought them downstairs.

I placed the vials on the kitchen counter and then moved as far away as possible. Even through the glass, the herb caused my eyes to water and my fingers to sting.

'Two eggs, then? They're in the larder behind you,' Cora directed.

I passed the eggs to her and she expertly cracked them in the bowl before taking the vervain out of the vial. She bit her lip and squinted at the bright-purple blossoms. 'Should I pretend they're berries? I'm not sure how many to put in.'

'Well, I guess as much as possible. Remember, humans can't taste vervain, so it doesn't matter,' I said.

'We can't take any chances or make any assumptions,' she said. 'Every part of a plan has a purpose. For all we know, he could simply kill the guards when he can't compel them. In which case, we need to make sure we bring stakes to attack. It won't be ideal, but it'll have to do.'

She had a point. Everything was important. I began to have the faintest glimmer of hope that this plan, as crazy as it was, might just work. 'How else can I help?' I asked.

'Just watch,' Cora said. 'I like having company in the kitchen. Violet and I always used to cook together.'

'I'm sorry,' I said automatically as soon as she mentioned Violet's name.

Cora turned to me, holding her spoon as if it were a weapon. Despite myself, I laughed at her serious demeanour.

'Stop it! You could say "I'm sorry" for eternity. But you didn't do any of this. Samuel did. And he'll be stopped.' As if to prove her point, she put the spoon down, picked up a knife and cleanly sliced through a block of butter.

Just then, the door burst open and Damon walked in. He was still in his tailcoat, but his bow tie was hanging loosely round his neck.

'Hello!' he said, walking into the kitchen and surveying the scene. 'What is this? Have we abandoned revenge to open up a bakery? How quaint!' His sarcasm didn't go unnoticed. He peered into Cora's bowl.

'None for you.' She swatted his hand away. 'Stefan and I have a plan.'

'All right, you've piqued my curiosity,' he said, sitting expectantly at the table as Cora scooped spoonfuls of the mixture onto a large baking tray.

'Samuel's next target is the prime minister's house, and presumably the prime minister himself. We're going to bring these vervain-laced biscuits to the guards at Downing Street, to protect them from compulsion, and ask them to deliver more biscuits to everyone inside. After that, we'll wait for Samuel and then make our move.'

'I'll go with you,' Damon said, surprising me with his willingness. 'In case things start to go sour, I'll be there to compel whomever necessary.'

'All right, then. That's why I'm glad you're here,' Cora said kindly as she pushed the baking tray into the oven. Soon, the air was filled with the sweet scent of biscuits. The plan could have been brilliant, or it could have been desperate. None of us had any idea how it would play out. But no matter what, we were all in it together.

* * *

The next afternoon, we followed Cora towards the prime minister's house. She was carrying a basket of biscuits. Above us, the sun was sinking low in the sky, but the air was warmer than it had been lately. I hoped the fine weather was a good omen. I needed something to believe in.

As we approached Ten Downing Street, I saw two fur-hatted guards standing to attention next to a simple gate. I glanced up, expecting to see a castle-like structure. But the prime minister's home was a modest brick building even smaller than the Bedford Square house we'd taken residence in.

We paused behind a tree on the opposite side of the street.

'Are we clear on the plan?' I asked.

Cora nodded, and I noticed her fingers holding the basket handle were trembling. At least Damon would be going with her.

'All right. Good luck,' I said. My heart was pounding, even though we weren't doing anything near as dangerous as we had in Miller's Court.

'Hello there!' Cora called across the pavement, swinging her basket as though she were Little Red Riding Hood from the fairy tale. Only our tale was far more horrific. I shook my head. *Focus, Stefan.*

The guards stood to attention. 'Yes, miss?' Their gaze

cut to Damon suspiciously.

'I brought you biscuits, something to say thank you for your service,' Cora said sweetly, trying to distract their attention from Damon.

'That's very nice of you, miss,' said one of the guards. 'But I'm afraid we can't accept gifts. I'm sure you understand.'

Damon smoothly stepped in front of Cora, ready to compel. 'My sister baked biscuits for Mr Cecil and his staff. She would be most obliged if you would take them, eat what you'd like and then distribute the rest.'

'All right,' the guard said slowly, reaching for the basket. 'If you insist.'

'Wait!' a tall guard called from across the street, marching towards the front door. 'Can't just take anything that's given. It's orders to refuse it all. Can't be too careful.'

Damon swivelled toward this guard, locking eyes. 'Take one,' he snapped. He was losing his patience. I hoped he would keep control long enough to get Cora out of there safely.

'Of course. As you were!' The guard saluted his colleagues and turned to take the basket.

'Thank you!' Cora curtsied as the basket was lifted from her hands. The guard took a large bite, a vacant expression on his face as he stared into the distance and chewed.

'Give my regards to the prime minister!' Cora called over

her shoulder. The guard nodded as crumbs rained down into his bushy black beard.

Damon and Cora nodded to each other, partners in crime, as they turned to meet me behind the tree. We weren't especially hidden, but the street was crowded and the guards seemed busier posing for delighted tourists' entertainment than protecting the door.

'It worked,' Cora breathed.

'Not yet.' Damon set his jaw. 'That's our insurance policy. But we need a main event so we can cash in. We need Samuel to come so we can end this once and for all.'

I slid to the base of the tree and continued to watch the house from a gap in the bushes.

We didn't have to wait long. As soon as the sun had set and every streaky orange ray had disappeared from the sky, an elegant carriage rode up to the entrance, pulled by two pitch-black horses. Samuel's coach.

The driver jumped down and set a stool alongside the edge of the passenger car. In a moment, two women stepped out, followed by Lord Ainsley and Samuel. The two women were well dressed, but I didn't recognise them from the party the night before. I wondered whether they were down-on-their-luck girls from the East End or noblewomen, and then realised it didn't matter. They were vampires, and vampires crossed all class lines.

'Are you a good girl, Molly?' Samuel asked, caressing the neck of one of the girls.

'I am *your* good girl,' Molly responded in a sing-song voice. She hungrily licked her lips, a clear sign she was ready to feed on anything or anyone.

'And what about you, Josephine?' he asked the other girl lecherously. He was showing off for Lord Ainsley, but I also sensed he enjoyed the act of compelling. That was a difference that made him truly inhuman.

'I'll do anything you ask,' she purred, lurching towards him and throwing her arms round him.

'I'm glad to hear it from both of you,' Samuel said, gently prying Josephine's arms from his neck. 'But only one of you can be my new right-hand woman. I've devised a little test. Would you girls like to hear it?'

Molly nodded eagerly.

'Terrific. Whoever can get inside and have Mr Robert Cecil come to the door and invite me in will receive a very fine reward indeed. Now go. Make me proud,' he said, sending them both off with a tap on each of their backs.

Molly turned and practically skipped towards the guards. She was humming under her breath, and any casual observer would assume she was drunk. Josephine slowly followed after her, glowering the whole way.

Samuel turned back to Lord Ainsley and smiled, as though they were his two prize show ponies being sent into the ring. 'Lesson number one, Ainsley. Get the girls to fight each other. One of them will get us invited inside. Because the only thing more fearsome than a vampire is two female vampires with something to prove.' The two men guffawed as hatred welled within me. I wanted to spring forward now and tear Samuel limb from limb. I wanted to pluck his heart from his chest with my bare hands, then parade it around town.

'Coward!' Damon hissed. I'm sure he was having similar revenge fantasies.

Cora shook her head, then held her hands together as if in prayer.

The two women approached the guards, neither of them seeming especially aware of the fact that this was the prime minister's home or that it required more security than a simple residence.

'Hold up!' a guard called, raising his arm towards Molly.

'I need to get in,' she said slowly. Each word was over-enunciated. The guard's gaze flicked to his partner, then locked on to her. I held my breath. The vervain would protect the guard from compulsion. But what would Samuel do when he realised they'd been dosed? It wouldn't take long.

Cora gripped my arm so tightly her nails dug into my skin.

Quickly realising her Power wasn't working, Molly made her exit and shuffled back to the waiting coach. Josephine seized her opportunity and ran, shrieking, up the path to the guards. 'Help! Please! I need help!'

'What's the matter, miss?' the guard asked, focusing his attention on Josephine.

'I'm being chased!' she said in a breathy voice. 'This man has been running after me for miles – I'm afraid he's the Ripper! Please, help me.'

The guards turned to each other and had a hushed conversation before one of them stepped aside and nodded to Josephine.

A crack of thunder followed by scattered drops of rain sealed the decision.

'All right, come in,' he offered, opening the door and ushering her inside.

The door closed with a thud. Damon and I locked eyes. Josephine had got in, and there was nothing my brother or I could do about it.

'Cora, you'll have to go in after her. Stefan and I won't be able to compel our way inside without an invitation,' Damon said under his breath.

Cora nodded, but she was visibly nervous. I grabbed her

hand and squeezed it once to comfort her, before we stealthily made our way along the line of bushes towards the back of the house. Samuel's hawklike gaze was trained on the front door, so we slipped by unnoticed. Around the perimeter of the lawn, large plants were covered with heavy burlap sacks to protect them from the frost. In the darkness, the covered plants looked like tombstones.

'I'll get rid of the guard,' Damon said tersely as he brushed the dirt off his hands and strode up to the man protecting the back entrance. Midway up the slate path, he locked eyes with him.

'You need to leave this post,' he said.

'Who are you, sir?' The man squinted suspiciously at Damon as he reached for the truncheon that hung by his side. The compulsion wasn't working.

Without bothering to answer, Damon charged towards him at vampire speed and knocked him to the ground, his head smashing into the stone. His body fell limp.

Cora's hand flew to her mouth in fear. 'Is he dead?' she asked.

'No,' I said, hoping that was the truth. I squinted and saw the man's chest rising and falling. He was merely unconscious.

I raced up the garden path with Cora, not wanting to waste another second. I was simultaneously horrified and impressed by Damon's quick actions. I sometimes forgot that we didn't always need to rely on magic or compulsion to get what we wanted.

Another crack of thunder sounded, and Damon quickly punched a downstairs window in the midst of the noise. Somewhere in the distance a dog barked. Damon turned to us, his eyes wild.

'You don't have much time,' he said, grabbing a fallen tree branch and cracking it over his knee. He handed it to Cora. 'Go in and kill the vampire. And then we'll kill Samuel.'

I shot him a look. Leave it to Damon to be as delicate about our situation as possible.

'Cora.' I turned to her. 'You'll be great. You're strong. But if there's any hint of danger, promise me you'll run right back here. We can figure out another way.'

She nodded resolutely and hoisted herself through the broken window.

'And now the games *really* begin.' Damon slid into a seated position next to me. He rifled through his pocket until he found a small pouch of chewing tobacco. 'Want some?' he asked, as if we were just two men whiling away the hours.

I shook my head silently, all attention and Power focused on Cora inside the house.

'Suit yourself,' he said, putting a large wad in his mouth. 'Aren't you proud of me, brother? Going along with this whole "saving the prime minister" plan? Even if it might be among your most ridiculous.'

'I don't really care what you think,' I murmured reflexively.

'Stefan.' Damon shook his head. 'Always wanting to get the last word in.' He chuckled.

'Right,' I said shortly. 'Let's just focus on Cora and the task at hand. Shouldn't we protect people while we still can?'

He shrugged. 'We're vampires, Stefan, not gods. We're merely death's messengers.'

That was the difference between me and my brother. I believed we did have a choice. We may have been meant to die that night in Mystic Falls. But certainly, all our victims over the past few decades weren't fated to be food and Power for monsters.

I cocked my head, trying to listen for any sound within the house. But there was nothing beyond hushed murmurs, beating hearts and clinking dishes – the sounds of a house that had no idea what was going on within its very walls.

I rose to my knees and peeked through the window into what appeared to be a small library. Shelves of books lined the room, two leather club chairs were set up so they faced each other, and a looking glass in the far corner of the room reflected my expression: I was pale with red veins visible under my skin.

Suddenly I heard a shriek, then racing footsteps. Soon Cora came into view. She dived out of the window, getting a cut on her upper arm in the process, and fell on top of me.

'Did you do it?' Damon asked roughly.

Cora nodded. 'We need to go. Get me out of here!'

Damon picked her up, slung her over his shoulder and ran away from the house at vampire speed. I tried to follow, but was pulled back by one of the guards who'd rushed round to the back of the house. He put two fingers in his mouth and whistled, causing five more guards to race over, pointing rifles at me.

And then, one of them turned and saw the prone body of the guard Damon had knocked unconscious. He was lying perfectly still, and from a distance he looked like a murder victim.

'Harry is dead!' the guard screamed. 'We're under attack!' A shot rang out.

I turned to face the circle of guards and bared my fangs, anything to buy Damon and Cora a few more minutes to escape. A ripple of panic spread through the group.

'Fire!' One of the guards shot his gun, and I bolted. A bullet grazed my shoulder as I ran at vampire speed into the darkness. Behind me, I could hear a shout: 'Stop that man!'

But they were too late.

CHAPTER 14

I fled down the streets, listening for the sound of Cora's heart. I could hear it, fast and jerky, and followed it until I found the source. Damon and Cora were sitting underneath the awning of a bakery, which provided little protection from the now pelting rain. Cora was lying in Damon's lap, sobbing.

'What happened?' I demanded. 'Is she all right?'

'Cora is. But the compelled vampire wasn't so lucky. Cora did a great job.'

I gingerly rubbed her back. She was crying into Damon's shirt and seemed oblivious to my presence. 'Cora, it's all right,' I said. 'You did exactly what we wanted.'

She turned and stared at me, tears running down her cheeks. Her expression looked as broken and terrified as it had after she killed Violet.

'Cora, you did everything you were supposed to. You're

safe. Now, what happened?' I asked, using my shirtsleeve to wipe the tears rolling down her cheeks.

'I killed the vampire,' she said in a low, monotone voice. 'I took the stake and I just reached back and stabbed her in the heart. And she shrieked, and then her whole body began *shrivelling* . . . it was awful.'

'She was just a vampire. She'd have killed you if given half a chance,' Damon said, clearly uncomfortable with playing the role of comforter.

'Like Violet was *just a vampire*?' Cora asked. 'Don't you see? I'm a killer now. And not only in self-defence, like it was with Violet. I went into that house for one reason, and one reason only. To kill that woman. And what was the point? Samuel's still on the loose. What I did seems so stupid right now.' She shook her head angrily.

'It wasn't stupid, it was necessary,' Damon said.

I nodded; I understood why Cora was so upset. There was something about that first kill that changes you, but it's how easy it is to murder again that is truly terrifying. As if the first time hadn't been just a fluke, but something you'd secretly enjoyed. I moved closer to Cora, putting my arm round her in what I hoped was a comforting embrace.

She pulled away from me and rose to her feet. 'I'm sorry if I disappointed you. I just need some time.' She turned and raced down an alley.

'Cora!' I called into the darkness.

'Don't.' Damon shook his head.

'We can't have her running around the city when there are vampires everywhere. I'll go and get her.'

'She needs some time, brother. And we need to turn around, go back to the prime minister's house and kill Samuel. Finish what we started.'

As I was about to answer, I heard the sound of footsteps, far too quick to be human, passing by the alley.

'Bloody disaster. Must have been those damned Salvatore brothers again. Meddling was not part of our deal. All bets are off now. I'll kill them both with my bare hands.'

'Quite right, Mortimer,' Lord Ainsley said.

'Can I have the girl?' Molly asked.

'Have the girl,' Samuel spat. 'She's caused me nothing but trouble. Her blood is spoiled for me.'

I turned to Damon. Without a word, he nodded to me, and we took off into the night, following the sound of Samuel's conversation. Soon, I realised, we were heading down to the warehouses on the water.

'A killer always comes back to the scene of a crime,' Damon said as we walked towards the low, squat wooden buildings where Samuel had first begun his reign of terror. We were too far back, keeping a safe distance, to know which warehouse they'd gone into. But I knew it would only be a matter of time before we found them.

Damon cocked his head and sniffed the air. 'Hold on,' he said. 'Always best to power up before a fight.' With that, he turned and sped off in the direction of several drunken revellers. Of course. Damon was going to drain the blood of some degenerate. I felt a surge in my veins and wondered if I should do the same. Damon was right: wasn't feeding just one way to prepare for the battle to come? But Samuel had already turned me into more of a monster than I'd been in twenty years, and I wasn't about to let him turn me into something worse.

Before I could start to second-guess myself, Damon returned.

'Brother,' he said curtly. The scent of hot, fresh blood wafted from his mouth, and it was all I could do to keep my fangs from making an appearance. 'Shall we?' he asked, indicating the warehouse where Samuel had hosted one of his famous dock parties.

I stepped onto a rotting crate and peered through a filthy window. A dozen people wandered around the room, wearing well-tailored clothes and looking as though they had made a wrong turn on the way to a ball. I knew they must be Samuel's vampires. In the centre of the warehouse was a pile of bodies. Blood still dripped from some of the wounds on their necks, like a fountain in the centre of a town square.

All of a sudden, one of the vampires turned towards me, fangs flashing. I jumped down, hoping I hadn't been spotted.

'Let me see.' Damon pushed me aside so he could look through the window. But it was too late. The window and door were suddenly smashed open, and two vampires barrelled out, pinning me to the dock as I desperately writhed under their crushing weight. Though newly turned, they were surprisingly strong, and every time I seemed to loosen one of my limbs, it would be pinned down again.

I heard a crash as another vampire jumped down through the broken window. The sound was followed by a snarl. I twisted my head to see Damon and Lord Ainsley locked in combat. Lord Ainsley was growling and gnashing his fangs as Damon struggled to wrestle him to the ground. Damon ended up flat on his back instead.

'Hold off, Ainsley!' Samuel's voice echoed as all the vampires looked up expectantly, as though he were a priest who'd just ascended an altar at a church service. 'And hold off on the brother, too. They're mine.'

He placed the heel of his boot on Damon's chest and leaned his weight into his foot. Damon gasped, and I heard the crunch of a rib breaking.

'Let this be a lesson to you,' Samuel said, glancing at the

vampires around him. More vampires had circled the two who'd pinned me down, and I could no longer see Samuel. All I could see were eight bloodthirsty vampires glaring at me, their newly formed murderous drive practically glowing in their eyes. 'Damon here is a vampire who might have made quite a good foot soldier at one point. He's smart. Devious. Charming. We could have been quite a team if he hadn't made some unfortunate blunders in his youth. He set his sights on women he didn't deserve. As if my long-ago love, Katherine, would ever truly have taken him seriously! But he persevered, only to kill carelessly. Not to mention choosing the wrong teammate.' At this, Samuel kicked Damon's ribs and stalked towards me, leaving him gasping for breath.

A shaft of moonlight fell on Samuel, giving him a sort of spotlight. At that moment, I had a feeling those eight vampires would have been easier to fight off than Samuel alone. He looked tall, refreshed and utterly triumphant. He was the hunter, and I was the felled prey. Samuel had two choices: kill or compel. I wasn't sure which would be the worse fate.

He knelt down until his face was only inches from mine. 'I'm done playing games.' He cupped my chin and forced me to look him in the eyes. I squeezed mine shut.

'Patrick!' he barked, and one of the young vampires

prised my eyelids open with his stubby fingers. I writhed, looking up at the stars, trying as hard as I could to pinpoint the constellations, anything that wasn't Samuel.

'Look at me!' he ordered, grabbing a fistful of my hair and pulling my head up from the wooden dock.

'No!' I averted my gaze and focused on a spot of dried blood on his cheek. What could I do to resist his compulsion? I tried to think of anything – Katherine, Mystic Falls, Cora, Violet – anything to take me to another time and place. I knew I had to resist looking into his eyes, but I felt my head being turned without my control, and I knew it would only be a matter of time before . . .

A blur raced toward Samuel, and a jolt caused him to release his grip. Damon had regained his strength and fought off Lord Ainsley. He jumped on Samuel's back, but before he could get a good hold on him, five more vampires piled on top of Damon and pulled him off, leaving Samuel free to reinstate his death grip on me.

'Your brother won't help you now, although your familial ties are admirable,' Samuel said. 'As you know, I had a brother once. And then you two murdered him. And I'm afraid I'm the type of man who holds a grudge. Terrible character flaw, I know, but luckily, I have an eternity to attempt to correct it.'

I bit the inside of my lip and continued to look up at the

sky. But then I felt a burning sensation on my skin and realised one of the young vampires was holding a lit match to my cheek as Samuel continued to hold me down. I involuntarily jerked my head and locked eyes with Samuel.

'Good.' He smiled. 'Just stay there, and the fire will be over before you know it. But if you resist, then we'll have to add more flames. It's your choice.' I could smell my burning flesh and feel the flames heading towards my hairline. In the centre of Samuel's eyes, I was entranced by two tiny figures.

'That's it,' he murmured, his voice sounding as though he was talking underwater. 'Now, your brother was never good to you, was he? Always disappointed you? Always caused trouble?'

I couldn't break my gaze. In Samuel's left eye, I immediately recognised Damon. Or, at least, Damon's body, consumed by flames. And in the right eye was a version of me. I was with a woman — whether I was kissing her or feeding from her neck, I wasn't quite sure.

Was that the past? Was it the future? I didn't know, but I was transfixed, wanting to see more. Samuel was still speaking, but I barely listened. All that existed in my mind was an image of Damon, dead.

'You may have turned your brother into a vampire, but he's been the one to kill you, countless times. He's destroyed your soul. And the only thing left to do is to destroy him.' I nodded, almost unbidden as the image in Samuel's eyes began to morph, and suddenly Damon was the one bent over the woman, *his* lips on her neck, brushing away her red hair. And I knew who the woman was. Callie.

The flames were getting hotter, and all of a sudden I was no longer on the dock. I was back in New Orleans, on a hot, sticky September night. I was about to kiss Callie, when she staggered into me, a knife sticking out of her back. I lunged towards Damon, but I was too late. Callie was dead, but I still wanted more than anything to destroy Damon. I knew it wouldn't bring her back to life, but it would give me the closure I so desperately craved. So Damon despised me for turning him into a vampire? Fine. Then let me kill him and be done with it.

But going after innocent people just to torture me? To prove some point about what happened in the past? I had wanted to kill Damon, then, back when he'd stabbed Callie. But I hadn't. I'd held off. Deep down, I'd thought maybe something would change. Deep down, I'd thought I'd regret killing my brother. But some people didn't deserve a chance. I thought of how Cora had killed Violet. She'd cried, but she'd realised that the creature she killed wasn't truly her sister. Why couldn't I do the same?

Samuel must have sensed my vulnerability. He knelt down next to me and whispered in a low voice, 'Kill Damon.'

'Kill Damon,' I repeated. It felt as if a cloud had lifted from my mind, and everything suddenly clicked together with unflinching clarity. It was so simple. I couldn't believe it had taken me so long to realise what I had to do to finally feel free. I had to kill my brother.

If Damon were dead, I wouldn't have to wonder who he was torturing, or being tortured by. I wouldn't have to worry about his moods, or his temper, or his tendency to laugh in the face of death. Most important, I wouldn't have to worry if Damon was going to turn on me and kill me at any given moment. If Damon were dead, I wouldn't have to worry at all.

I looked Samuel directly in the eyes, a smile forming on my face.

He handed me a stake. 'You know what you have to do.'

I did. The whole time I'd been in London, I'd been fighting the wrong enemy. The enemy was Damon. Now I had a new mission: destroy my brother.

CHAPTER 15

I frantically searched the docks for my brother – my prey. Damon had overtaken two young vampires. One was lying on his back, his head at an unnatural angle, while the other had a stake protruding from his chest.

Adrenalin throbbed in my veins. But it was odd: it was as if my energy was pulling *for* Damon rather than against him. For the past few weeks, whenever I saw him in the middle of a battle, I'd feel my Power surge as though it could leap from my veins to his. I wasn't sure if it ever worked.

No, that was wrong. I didn't want to help Damon. I glanced again at his victims. These would be my brother's last murders. I would make sure of that. More vampires were circling him, but none had attacked. It was clear they were bound to whatever Samuel said and wouldn't go in for the kill until given the instruction.

'Stand clear!' Samuel commanded. The vampires stepped

even further away, opening up a path to my brother. I walked steadily towards Damon, hatred surging in my veins and overriding any instinctual inclination to help him. Yes, he had been my brother, but that was a lifetime ago. It was time to finally cut the filial ties. I'd be better off. With each footstep, I came up with new reasons to hate him. *He worked tirelessly to steal Katherine from me. He killed Callie. He forced me into marriage in New York. He'd killed hundreds, perhaps thousands, of innocent people. He promised me an eternity of misery for turning him into a vampire, when all I'd wanted was my brother by my side.*

We were face-to-face. I saw his blue eyes flicker towards me.

'Brother?' Damon asked.

Hatred flared in me. I hated the way he said it, so territorial and possessive. As if being brothers allowed infinite betrayals. How dare he stand in front of me, so cocky and self-assured? How dare he not apologise for the hell he'd put me through ever since Katherine had come to Mystic Falls?

'Stefan?' he asked tentatively. There was a note of something I hadn't often heard in his voice. It was fear.

'You deserve to be frightened,' I said quietly. 'Because this battle is personal, and I won't forgive you for anything. Not until I've drained you of every last drop of blood in your body.' Before he could respond, I lunged at him, wresting the stake from his hands.

'Brother?' Damon asked again, this time in confusion, attempting to twist out of my grip. 'You're being compelled. Stefan, this isn't you. This is Samuel, the one you've been fighting for weeks. Don't let him win, don't let him do this to you.'

'No, Damon. That's where you're wrong. This is all I've thought about for the past twenty years. Now I finally have my chance.' I raised the stake and was about to plunge it into Damon's chest when he shoved me away, sending the stake flying from my grasp. I pushed him back and we began wrestling on the dock. A remote part of my brain registered that we used to wrestle like this as children, testing our strength in the grounds of Veritas. But we weren't children any more.

'Stefan, you don't know what you're doing,' Damon said, an edge of panic rising in his voice. 'If you're going to kill me, kill me as Stefan Salvatore, not as one of Samuel's minions.' His face was red, and sweat was beading on his temples.

'This is who I am, *brother*.' The stake was still a few feet out of reach. Around us, the ring of vampires watched the fight. Blind rage overtook me. I'd rip Damon's heart out with my hands if I had to.

'Come on, Stefan. Show your brother who's boss.' Samuel's smooth voice rose over the crowd. He reached down and handed me the stake. I pulled it back and aimed it at the centre of Damon's heart. I couldn't wait to see his blood, rich and red thanks to all his conquests, spill onto the dock. I couldn't wait for his limp, lifeless body to be thrown into the Thames.

'Goodbye forever,' I growled. I used the stake to pop off one of the buttons on his shirt, then gently scratched his skin. Blood spurted from the wound.

'If you do this, you'll regret it for eternity, and that's a promise,' he said, pushing me off him. He'd been holding off from truly fighting me, I realised, thinking that he'd be able to talk me out of killing him. It just showed how little he knew me.

I quickly jumped on him, pinning him back down. He was stronger than me, but I had adrenalin and twenty years of hatred surging in my veins. There was no way he'd get away from me again. I pushed his shoulders into the dock.

'Stefan, don't do this. I swear, you'll hate yourself more than you already do if you go through with it.' I wasn't listening. I closed my eyes and pulled the stake back until a crack of lightning lit up the night sky, illuminating Damon's face. Just then, fire sprang up from a spot on the dock and quickly formed a ring around us. I heard shrieks and whirled round in confusion and anger. Why was there a fire? I had important work to do.

That's when I saw Cora running towards us, her hair loose and wild around her face. Behind her was Lady Alice. It was a shock to my system to see anyone other than Damon. It didn't feel as though they belonged in this world, in this place of battle.

Lady Alice lifted her hands to the sky and began chanting a low, guttural *ah* sound over and over again.

'Samuel?' I called in confusion. The fire had circled around Damon and me, and I couldn't see an easy way to escape without burning myself and losing my grip on Damon. Was this a trap? Were *both* of us destined to die? I couldn't tell if Lady Alice had set the fire or was trying to stop it. Based on our last conversation, I assumed the former.

'Put down the stake,' Damon breathed, bringing me back to the task at hand. He was struggling against my grasp, and I knew it would only be a few seconds before he wrestled free.

'No.' I shook my head and clutched the stake tighter. But I looked over my shoulder, and Samuel was no longer watching us. Instead, he was pinned against the wall by an invisible force. Lady Alice was pointing her finger towards him.

'Stupid witch!' he yelled. 'You're ruining everything.'

'No, I'm making things right,' she said. 'I believe in an eye for an eye.'

Samuel squirmed under whatever spell Lady Alice was using to keep him glued to the building. He seemed far less powerful than I'd ever seen him before. Lady Alice turned her face to the sky and began chanting again, a loud sound that matched the thunder rumbling all around us. All of a sudden, the flames that had encircled us leaped like a fireball through the sky and against the wall of the warehouse, silhouetting Samuel.

'*Exuro in abyssus*,' Lady Alice shouted. The sky lit up with hundreds of lightning bolts, but the driving rain stopped. Then the warehouse burst into flames, igniting Samuel's body like a firecracker. The vampires on the dock fell to their knees under an invisible force. Was Samuel dead? Had Lady Alice just saved us all?

Samuel's charred body fell to the dock in a heap. The fire quickly spread, killing every one of Samuel's vampires in its wake. Lady Alice continued to chant until all of them had been burned to an unrecognisable state. The scent of smouldering flesh permeated the air.

I stood shakily. Several feet away, my brother was lying on the ground, his chest exposed and bloody.

Kill him.

I wasn't sure where the voice was coming from. It was like

a half-remembered dialogue in a nightmare. Kill Damon? I couldn't. Even the thought made my stomach turn in revulsion.

I looked down. Flecks of blood were on my hands, and there was an indentation where I'd gripped the stake. What had just happened? Had I actually tried to kill my brother? Samuel's compulsion must have been broken with his death. I turned to look at Damon, guilt filling my conscience. I was a monster capable of almost anything, but I could never have killed my brother. He leaned over and grabbed the stake, throwing it in the Thames. I pulled the sleeve from my shirt, intending to use it to staunch the blood from Damon's wound. I moved towards him, and our eyes locked. There was something flickering in his eyes that I'd never seen before. It was terror.

In the distance, police bells sounded. The entire dock was on fire. My head was pounding in the smoke, my feet felt disconnected from my body and I couldn't comprehend how I'd come so close to killing Damon.

Then suddenly everything faded to black.

CHAPTER 16

I woke on a white eiderdown blanket. The sun-dappled mahogany table next to me was laden with several vases of flowers. I turned my head on the pillow, trying to get my bearings. The room was far too luxurious to be my simple abode at Abbott Manor, and yet the bed and the night table were delicate, not at all like the rough-hewn furniture at Veritas. Suddenly, warm water was being dabbed on my forehead. I blinked. Above me sat a woman wearing a white gown. Was she an angel? The image swam into focus, and I realised it was Lady Alice.

'The fire,' I croaked as images from the night before sprang back into my mind. My throat hurt.

'Shh, just keep quiet. You swallowed quite a bit of smoke and ash. This is a rosemary poultice. It should calm you a little,' she said.

I struggled to a sitting position. 'What happened? Why

are you here?'

'You had a nasty run-in with Samuel and he tried to make you kill your brother,' Lady Alice explained matter-of-factly as she picked up a tin cup and brought it to my lips. I turned away, unsure what she might be giving me – or what she thought I deserved.

'It's just goat's blood. Cora said it was your favourite,' she said gently, again bringing the cup to my lips. This time, I drank, slowly, allowing the familiar liquid to run down my throat.

'Where's Damon?' I finally croaked, pushing the cup away.

'He's safe. He's back at Bedford Square. I brought you to my house to heal.' A heavy silence fell between us as I realised the enormity of what she'd done. She'd saved me *and* invited me – a vampire – into her home. I didn't know what to say.

'Why did you help?' I said finally.

'I realised I didn't have much of a choice,' Lady Alice said. 'Cora came running to me, begging me to intervene. She told me you were all in over your heads with Samuel. I eventually agreed, but by the time we got to the prime minister's house, you were long gone. Luckily, I was able to perform a locator spell.'

'But why now?'

'I had a talk with some wise witches, and I realised that if

Samuel had his way, evil would win. And then I'd lose. I'd already lost Mary Jane. I knew I couldn't lose anything else. And I came just in time,' she said.

'Thank you,' I said softly. It wasn't nearly enough. But what else could I say to the woman who not only saved my life but my brother's life, too?

'Don't thank me,' she said. 'Just prove to me I did the right thing. I saved you, and I expect a good turn from you one of these days. All our kind does. Promise me that.'

'I promise,' I said. After all our disagreements, Lady Alice and I really did want the same things.

'Enough about me. There are a few people here who want to see you. I'll let them know you're awake.'

Who could it be? Damon, I was sure, must hate me again.

I was surprised when Jemima, Gus, Billy and Vivian, the four orphans from Mary Jane's slum, walked in and surrounded my bed.

'They helped me reconsider. We all made mistakes when we tried to fight Samuel the first time, but Mary Jane would have wanted to help you. *Did* help you,' Lady Alice explained. 'And their presence has added strength to our coven. They're young, they're strong and they're hungry. That spell I performed down at the docks wasn't just coming from me. All the orphans were behind it as well. And that was enough to defeat Samuel and his vampire army. As soon as I realised the orphans didn't have anywhere to live besides the slum, I invited them to join me at my house. I hope Mary Jane would be happy,' Lady Alice said sadly.

'She would,' I assured her. Then I turned my attention to the orphans. 'Thank you for helping me, especially after everything that happened.'

'I hope we can put it all behind us,' Vivian said.

'We have the chance to change history,' Lady Alice said. 'Vampires and witches don't work together. And maybe for the most part it's better that way. But we all know now that sometimes, in extraordinary circumstances, witches and vampires can accomplish amazing things together.'

I smiled at the sentiment. I was feeling much stronger now, thanks to these kind witches. I swung my legs to the side of the bed and rose unsteadily to my feet.

'Thank you.' I wanted to tell them how sorry I was for the havoc Samuel had wreaked, and how I knew saving me didn't make them feel any better about losing Mary Jane. But I didn't. The situation was too much for words.

'You won't have to worry about me any more,' I said finally. 'I'll be moving on.'

'Good for you, then,' Jemima said. 'Good luck with everything.' I could tell that she actually meant it.

'Where will you go?' Gus asked.

'Maybe Australia,' I said, choosing a country at random. I

wanted to get away from rain, and death, and that seemed far enough away for a fresh start.

'You need protection. Here, let me,' Lady Alice murmured. She circled her hands around my head several times in quick succession. By the third time, the burned-out candles strewn around the floor lit up.

'*Ad lucem eterna,*' she intoned, and the younger witches took up the chorus. 'That will help keep your true identity a secret when evil comes.'

'Thank you,' I said. I knew a million thank-yous wouldn't express my gratitude for everything they'd done over these past few days.

A little while later, I said goodbye to the witches and readied myself to go. Just as I was about to leave, Cora walked in.

'Hi,' she said shyly.

'Hello.' I felt shy myself.

'You're just in time. Stefan's ready to leave,' Lady Alice said.

'Thank you for all you've done. And know that I won't forget Mary Jane.' I knew the promise wasn't enough to heal the ache in Lady Alice's heart.

'Please don't. And remember, you do have the potential to be a good man. But the tricky part is getting yourself to believe it.' She smiled sadly.

'I'll try,' I promised. Cora and I left the house and found ourselves back on London's bustling streets. Fruit and vegetable carts clamoured for space in the narrow lanes, ladies of the night were walking the pavements with rouged cheeks and low-cut dresses despite the early hour, and pub doors were flung open, welcoming thirsty labourers looking for a lunchtime pint. We could live here and set up house in Bedford Square. And yet I knew that was impossible.

Cora sighed, and I wondered if she was thinking the same thing.

'It's time for me to move on,' she said.

'I think that's a wonderful idea,' I told her.

'Damon's arranging passage for me to America later today. Will you see me off?'

'Of course,' I said.

It was odd that we'd most likely never see each other again. It was necessary for Cora's safety and for her well-being – as I'd learned, no good could come from a mortal spending time with a vampire. We lived on the same earth, but existed in two different worlds.

I reached into my pocket and pulled out Mr Sutherland's watch, which I'd been carrying ever since I left New York. It was tarnished with age and had a tiny bloodstain on it, but it continued to tick. It was a testament to time, nothing else. But it reminded me that this second was the only thing in life – vampire or mortal – that was ever truly certain.

I took Cora's hand and dropped the heavy timepiece in her palm. 'I'd like you to have this,' I said.

She examined it. 'Why are you giving it to me?' she asked in disbelief.

'You deserve it. To remind you that we shared time together and that it profoundly changed us both. And also to remind you that I will think of you, and remember you, for eternity,' I said. It was true.

'I'll miss you,' she said sadly.

'You'll be all right. You're the smartest, fiercest person I know. Remember that,' I said urgently.

Cora nodded. 'Thank you. I'll keep this forever, and never forget.'

We walked for a few minutes in silence, lost in our thoughts.

'I think when I get to America, I'll change my name. A true fresh start. I won't have had a sister. I won't have moved from London. I'll be from Ireland, seeking fame and fortune . . .' She trailed off, lost in the fantasy.

'Don't lie,' I said urgently. 'You might think it's easier, but it's not. Lies always come back. May I make a suggestion?'

'Of course,' she said.

'Go to Mystic Falls. It's the town Damon and I grew up in. It's beautiful. My father always used to call it God's country,' I said, remembering.

Cora smiled. 'That's what my father always said about Ireland, too!' she burst out.

I smiled. 'There's still one family in Mystic Falls who will help you. The Bennetts. Emily Bennett was a loyal friend who took good care of me, and she's a witch. Tell her family what happened. I know they'll protect you. And that way, you'll have someone to talk to about everything. Someone who might understand.'

'That would be nice,' she said in a small voice.

I glanced down at my ring, glinting in the sun. It was my ticket to freedom, the accessory that allowed me to walk in sunlight, among humans.

Just then, Big Ben began striking the hour. Ten o'clock.

Cora turned to me, her eyes wide. 'I should go. Damon said the ship leaves at four, but from Southampton. We're taking a train there.'

I knew I'd promised to see her off, but running into Damon again might not be the best thing for either of us right now. Not when I'd just tried to kill him. But even with the events of last night, I knew I needed to say goodbye to my brother.

A cab stopped at the kerb.

'Where you off to?' the coachman asked, genially tipping his hat to us.

'Bedford Square,' I said, opening the door for Cora and following her inside. It was a relief to take a cab through the streets in daylight, without relying on compulsion or scanning the crowd in fear of Samuel. The sun shone through the window, leaving a pattern of light on the black leather of the seat. I glanced out of the window as London rolled past me. The city would be all right. Cora would be all right. And, I realised, I'd be all right. I'd move somewhere else and hope that finally, this time, I'd stay out of trouble.

The driver stopped in front of the house and I sighed, wistful for all that might have been. In another world, could Cora and Damon and I have lived in happiness and solitude here? Could Damon and I have ever stopped bickering? No, I thought, trying desperately to push those questions out of my mind forever. It did no good to wonder. Because there *wasn't* another world. There was this world, and I had to live in it as a vampire.

'Sir?' the coach driver asked, and I realised he was standing with the door open, waiting for me to step out. I jumped down and offered my arm to Cora. She took it, and together we walked into the house.

CHAPTER 17

The sky above the ocean was a beautiful pink that reminded me of the magnolia trees when they were in full bloom back in Mystic Falls. It was the perfect contrast to the deep, moody blue of the Atlantic.

Damon and I glanced at each other. I still hadn't said anything about the fact that I'd almost killed him. I knew I'd been compelled to do it, but there was something deeper than that, too, and it shamed me. In that moment, I'd *wanted* Damon's death. And a tiny kernel in the depths of my being still did. Of course I'd never act on it, but being reminded it was there was unsettling, and a good reason why I couldn't continue to spend time with him.

'I guess this is it,' Cora said, glancing at the huge ship silhouetted against the sinking sun. She was dressed in a sky-blue dress, with a mink stole she'd found in the closet of the house in Bedford Square. Behind her, Damon was pulling a steamer trunk filled with everything she could fit in from the house, including a large chest of gold coins. She was a wealthy woman now, and I had no doubt she'd have no problems settling in America. Cora clutched her ticket in her hand: first class, one way, on the White Star line. 'Are you sure you don't want to come?'

I shook my head sadly. I didn't want to follow Cora, trailing behind her like a cloud always ready to break and unleash a torrent of terror.

'Small-town life was never right for me,' Damon said. 'I need to get a proper taste of Europe.' He picked her up and squeezed her tightly. 'Be good. I don't want to hear any reports of funny business in America. No killing vampires, no dressing up and infiltrating your way into charitable societies, and no becoming friends with any other creatures of darkness, you hear?'

Cora raised an eyebrow. 'Oh, like you'll just be waiting around for news from me. I know you'll be far too busy capturing the hearts of all the ladies of Europe. I just hope you eventually settle down!'

Then she turned to me. 'Stefan, thank you for everything,' she said seriously. 'And remember, no more apologies.'

'I'll try,' I said. Of course, that would mean that I'd have to stop doing things I regretted. Maybe I could.

'And both of you, take care of each other,' she said sternly.

'We will,' I said hollowly. Right now, it seemed the best way to take care of each other was to be as far away from each other as possible.

'Take care of me?' Damon protested. 'I think I need a bodyguard to make sure he doesn't go off the rails. He was terrifying! I'll tell you something, brother,' he said, slugging me companionably on my arm. I guess he wasn't as mad at me as I'd thought. Had we really moved past our petty differences? 'You're stronger than I thought. Why not use it? Just think, the two Salvatores could put on a real show, the kind that Gallagher and his circus could only dream of,' he said.

'I'm afraid I'm only up to doing battle once every twenty-five years,' I joked.

'So that would be, what? 1913? Cora, put it on your calendar. Wherever we are, we'll make sure you come to witness it,' Damon joked.

'I'm planning to be *quite* at peace in 1913, thank you very much,' she retorted. 'After all, I'll be a middle-aged lady by then. The lot of you wouldn't even look twice at me.'

'I'll make an exception,' Damon said, bowing deeply.

I imagined her twenty-five years in the future. She'd have a husband and children. I wondered if she'd name one of them Violet and tell them stories of their long-lost aunt's beauty and bravery. I wondered what else she'd tell them about the events that had made her the woman she'd become.

'But you've got me thinking,' Cora said spontaneously as the ship belched out three long, low horn blasts, a signal that departure was imminent. 'Why *not* meet in 1913? Wherever we are. I'll make sure if I move I'll always keep my address updated at the Mystic Falls post office. Somehow, you'll always be able to find me!' she said excitedly, her eyes full of hope that there was a future for her; a future for all of us. I nodded slowly. Maybe a meeting twenty-five years in the future would be enough for me to keep hope.

'Is it a deal, brother?' Damon asked, his face twisted into a smirk. I nodded slowly. For once, we weren't fighting over a girl. Instead, we were both able to let her ago, and she – and we – were all better off for it.

'Until then, gentlemen!' Cora said. She pulled out her pocket watch and reverentially touched it, then turned and walked up the gangplank. When she reached the end, she whirled round and blew us a kiss before disappearing onto the ship.

'Well, we did it,' Damon said, sounding as proud as if he were a parent sending his daughter down the aisle at her wedding.

'She did it,' I said. 'She's quite a girl.'

'We always do agree on the essential truths,' he said. 'So

now, where to? I've heard there's a wicked poker game that takes place at the Mouse Trap, just by the port. Shall we go all-in, like old times?' he asked, wiggling his eyebrows. 'You need to win some money to pay me back for the fact that you almost killed me.'

I shook my head. 'I'm leaving, too,' I explained.

Surprise crossed Damon's face. 'With Cora? Was that your plan?' he asked accusingly.

'No. I don't know where I'm going. I'll take whatever ship comes. Africa? Australia?'

'Are you sure? Because Europe is ours for the taking. We could have parties and balls and marry princesses from the Continent. We'd ensure that the Salvatore name would matter. That's my plan. Come and join me.'

I shook my head. For a split second, Damon looked disappointed. But it quickly passed.

'Probably for the best,' he said, pressing his lips into a straight line. 'I wouldn't want you cramping my style.'

I held out my hand for Damon to shake, but he ignored the gesture.

'Maybe in 1913,' I teased. He jammed his hands in his pockets and turned away without responding.

I watched his figure retreat down the pier, and then, when he was only a speck in the distance, I lifted my eyes to the horizon. The sun was sinking slowly. I glanced at the ships rocking in the sea, trying to decide which one to take.

My stomach rumbled, but I ignored it. There would be plenty of rats aboard whatever steamer I chose. I could live on rodents. It would be penance, and it would feel good after so much temptation. I'd taken money from the house, so I wouldn't have to worry about paying my fare. I wouldn't need to rely on compulsion. I wanted to start my next chapter with a clean slate. I would live a simple, and welcome, existence.

Cora's steamer lurched away, chugging towards the horizon. People on the deck blew kisses at the crowds that had congregated on the dock to wave goodbye. I tried to make out Cora, but I couldn't see her. I waved, still, bidding farewell to this chapter of my life as much as I was to Cora.

And then, once the ship had disappeared beyond the horizon, I turned and walked towards the town, shoulders squared, head up – just another man seeking a new life far away.

EPILOGUE

In one of my schoolbooks there was a painting called The Fountain of Youth, *an Edenic image of young, beautiful people in the middle of an endless party. As a child, I'd looked at it again and again, enchanted by the idea of immortality.*

Now I knew better. Immortality wasn't idyllic or enchanting. But it was powerful.

If I had to live forever, I had to make it count. And that was why I needed to get as far away as I could from temptation – and from Damon.

So that's why I boarded a ship bound for New Zealand. I had no idea if I'd stay for a month, a year or a century, and I liked it that way. I liked not needing a plan. I liked depending only on myself. And I liked the way it was so easy to slip into conversation with a stranger and no longer feel as though I was hiding a horrible secret.

I was Stefan Salvatore.

I still craved blood. The desire was relentless, all-consuming, a second heartbeat pounding away in the centre of my being. I wondered what it would feel like if I could just give in to my dark side, like Damon. I wondered what would have happened if Lady Alice hadn't come and saved both of us. When it mattered, in that final moment between life and death, would I have had the self-control to break the compulsion and pull myself off him?

I didn't think so.

And I vowed that for the rest of eternity, I'd never be in the position to find out.

THIRSTY FOR MORE?

~

TURN THE PAGE FOR A SNEAK PEEK AT

THE HUNTERS: MOONSONG

~

THE NEXT NOVEL IN THE ORIGINAL

Vampire Diaries

SERIES

CHAPTER 1

Dear Diary,

I'm so scared.

My heart is pounding, my mouth is dry, and my hands are shaking. I've faced so much and survived: vampires, werewolves, phantoms. Things I never imagined were real. And now I'm terrified. Why?

Simply because I'm leaving home.

And I know that it's completely, insanely ridiculous. I'm barely leaving home, really. I'm going to college, only a few hours' drive from this darling house where I've lived since I was a baby. No, I'm not going to start crying again. I'll be sharing a room with Bonnie and Meredith, my two best friends in the whole world. In the same dorm, only a couple of floors away, will be my beloved Stefan. My other best friend, Matt, will be just a short walk across campus. Even Damon will be in an apartment in the town nearby.

Honestly, I couldn't stick any closer to home unless I never moved out of this house at all. I'm being such a wimp. But it seems as if I've just got my home back – my family, my life – after being exiled for so long, and now I suddenly have to leave again.

I suppose I'm scared partly because these last few weeks of summer have been wonderful. We packed all the enjoyment we would have been having during these past few months – if it hadn't been for fighting the kitsune, travelling to the Dark Dimension, battling the jealousy phantom and all the other Extremely Not Fun things we've done – into three glorious weeks. We had picnics and sleepovers and went swimming and shopping. We took a trip to the county fair, where Matt won Bonnie a stuffed tiger and turned bright red when she squealed and leaped into his arms. Stefan even kissed me on the top of the Ferris wheel, just like any normal guy might kiss his girlfriend on a beautiful summer night.

We were so happy. So normal in a way I thought we could never be again.

That's what's frightening me, I guess. I'm scared that these few weeks have been a bright, golden interlude, and now that things are changing, we'll be heading back into darkness and horror. It's like that poem we read in English class last autumn says: Nothing gold can stay. Not for me.

Even Damon . . .

The clatter of feet in the hallway downstairs distracted her, and Elena Gilbert's pen slowed. She glanced up at the last couple of boxes scattered around her room. Stefan and Damon must be here to pick her up.

But she wanted to finish her thought, to express the last worry that had been nagging at her during these perfect weeks. She turned back to her diary, writing faster so that she could get her thoughts down before she had to leave.

Damon has changed. Ever since we defeated the jealousy phantom, he's been . . . kinder. Not just to me, not just to Bonnie, who he's always had a soft spot for, but even to Matt and Meredith. He can still be intensely irritating and unpredictable – he wouldn't be Damon without that – but he hasn't had that cruel edge to him. Not like he used to.

He and Stefan seem to have come to an understanding. They know I love them both, and yet they haven't let jealousy come between them. They're close, acting like true brothers in a way I haven't seen before. There's this delicate balance between the three of us that's lasted through the end of the summer. And I worry that any mis-step on my part will bring it crashing down and that like their first

love, Katherine, I'll tear the brothers apart. And then we'll
lose Damon forever.

Aunt Judith called up, sounding impatient, 'Elena!'

'Coming!' Elena replied. She quickly scribbled a few more
sentences in her diary.

Still, it's possible that this new life will be wonderful.
Maybe I'll find everything I've been looking for. I can't hold
on to high school, or to my life here at home, forever. And
who knows? Maybe this time the gold will stay.

'Elena! Your ride is *waiting*!'

Aunt Judith was definitely getting stressed out now. She'd
wanted to drive Elena up to school herself. But Elena knew
she wouldn't be able to say goodbye to her family without
crying, so she'd asked Stefan and Damon to drive her
instead. It would be less embarrassing to get emotional here
at home than to weep all over Dalcrest's campus. Since Elena
had decided to go with the Salvatore brothers, Aunt Judith
had been working herself up about every little detail,
anxious that Elena's college career wouldn't start off perfectly
without her there to supervise. It was all because Aunt Judith
loved her, Elena knew.

She slammed the blue-velvet-covered journal shut and

dropped it into an open box. She climbed to her feet and headed for the door, but before she opened it, she turned to look at her room one last time.

It was so empty, with her favourite posters missing from the walls and half the books gone from her bookcase. Only a few clothes remained in her dresser and closet. The furniture was all still in place. But now that the room was stripped of most of her possessions, it felt more like an impersonal hotel room than the cosy haven of her childhood.

So much had happened here. Elena could remember cuddling up with her father on the window seat to read together when she was a little girl. She and Bonnie and Meredith – and Caroline, who had been her good friend, too, once – had spent at least a hundred nights here telling secrets, studying, dressing for dances and just hanging out. Stefan had kissed her here, early in the morning, and disappeared quickly when Aunt Judith came to wake her.

Elena remembered Damon's cruel, triumphant smile as she invited him in that first time, what felt like a million years ago. And, not so long ago, her joy when he had appeared here one dark night, after they all thought he was dead.

There was a quiet knock at the door, and it swung open. Stefan stood in the doorway, watching her.

'About ready?' he said. 'Your aunt is a little worried. She thinks you're not going to have time to unpack before orientation if we don't get going.'

Elena stood and went over to wrap her arms around him. He smelled clean and woodsy, and she nestled her head against his shoulder. 'I'm coming,' she said. 'It's just hard to say goodbye, you know? Everything's changing.'

Stefan turned towards her and caught her mouth softly in a kiss. 'I know,' he said when the kiss ended, and ran his finger gently along the curve of her bottom lip. 'I'll take these boxes down and give you one more minute. Aunt Judith will feel better if she sees the truck getting packed up.'

'Okay. I'll be right down.'

Stefan left the room with the boxes, and Elena sighed, looking around again. The blue flowered curtains her mother had made for her when she was nine still hung over the windows. She remembered her mother hugging her, her eyes a little teary, when her baby girl told her she was too big for Winnie the Pooh curtains.

Elena's own eyes filled with tears, and she tucked her hair behind her ears, mirroring the gesture her mother had used when she was thinking hard. Elena was so young when her parents died. Maybe if they'd lived, she and her mother would be friends now, would know each other as equals, not just as mother and daughter.

Her parents had gone to Dalcrest College, too. That's where they'd met, in fact. Downstairs on top of the piano sat a picture of them in their graduation robes on the sun-filled lawn in front of the Dalcrest library, laughing, impossibly young.

Maybe going to Dalcrest would bring Elena closer to them. Maybe she'd learn more about the people they'd been, not just the mum and dad she'd known when she was little, and find her lost family among the neoclassical buildings and the sweeping green lawns of the college.

She wasn't leaving, not really. She was moving forward.

She set her jaw firmly and headed out of her room, clicking off the light as she went.

Downstairs, Aunt Judith, her husband, Robert, and Elena's five-year-old sister, Margaret, were gathered in the hall, waiting, watching Elena as she came down the stairs.

Aunt Judith was fussing, of course. She couldn't keep still; her hands were twisting together, smoothing her hair, or fiddling with her earrings. 'Elena,' she said, 'are you sure you've packed everything you need? There's so much to remember.' She frowned.

Her aunt's obvious anxiety made it easier for Elena to smile reassuringly and hug her. Aunt Judith held her tight, relaxing for a moment, and sniffed. 'I'm going to miss you, sweetheart.'

'I'll miss you, too,' Elena said, and squeezed her closer, feeling her own lips tremble. She gave a shaky laugh. 'But I'll be back. If I forgot anything, or if I get homesick, I'll run right back for a weekend. I don't have to wait for Thanksgiving.'

Next to them, Robert shifted from one foot to the other and cleared his throat. Elena let go of Aunt Judith and turned to him.

'Now, I know college students have a lot of expenses,' he said. 'And we don't want you to have to worry about money, so you've got an account at the student store, but . . .' He opened his wallet and handed her a fistful of bills. 'Just in case.'

'Oh,' Elena said, touched and a little flustered. 'Thank you so much, Robert, but you really don't have to.'

He patted her awkwardly on the shoulder. 'We want you to have everything you need,' he said firmly. Elena smiled at him gratefully, folded the money and put it in her pocket.

Next to Robert, Margaret glared down obstinately at her shoes. Elena knelt in front of her and took her little sister's hands. 'Margaret?' she prompted.

Large blue eyes stared into her own. Margaret frowned and shook her head, her mouth a tight line.

'I'm going to miss you so much, Meggie,' Elena said, pulling her close, her eyes filling with tears again. Her little sister's dandelion-soft hair brushed against Elena's cheek. 'But I'll be back for Thanksgiving, and maybe you can come and visit me on campus. I'd love to show off my little sister to all my new friends.'

Margaret swallowed. 'I don't want you to go,' she said in a small, miserable voice. 'You're always *leaving*.'

'Oh, sweetie,' Elena said helplessly, cuddling her closer. 'I always come back, don't I?'

Elena shivered. Once again, she wondered how much Margaret remembered of what had *really* happened in Fell's Church during the last year. The Guardians promised to change everyone's memories of those dark months when vampires, werewolves and kitsune had nearly destroyed the town – and when Elena herself had died and risen again – but there seemed to be exceptions. Caleb Smallwood remembered, and sometimes Margaret's innocent face looked strangely knowing.

'Elena,' Aunt Judith said again, her voice thick and weepy, 'you'd better get going.'

Elena hugged her sister one more time before letting her go. 'Okay,' she said, standing and picking up her bag. 'I'll call you tonight and let you know how I'm settling in.'

Aunt Judith nodded, and Elena gave her another quick kiss before wiping her eyes and opening the front door.

Outside, the sunlight was so bright she had to blink.

Damon and Stefan were leaning against the truck Stefan had rented, her stuff packed into the back. As she stepped forward, they both glanced up and, at the same time, smiled at her.

Oh. They were so beautiful, the two of them, that seeing them could still leave her shaken after all this time. Stefan, her love Stefan, his leaf-green eyes shining at the sight of her, was gorgeous with his classical profile and that sweet little kissable curve to his bottom lip.

And Damon – all luminescent pale skin, black velvety eyes and silken hair – was graceful and deadly all at once. His brilliant smile made something inside her stretch and purr like a panther recognising its mate.

Both pairs of eyes watched her lovingly, possessively.

The Salvatore brothers were hers now. What was she going to do about it? The thought made her frown and made her shoulders hunch nervously. Then she consciously smoothed the wrinkles in her forehead away, relaxed and smiled back at them. What would come, would come.

'Time to go,' she said, and tilted her face up towards the sun.

CHAPTER 1

Adam's car windows were foggy with the heat of their breath. It was a balmy night at dusk, and the air was scented with early signs of spring – a perfect night to roll down the windows and enjoy the breeze while they kissed. But Cassie insisted the windows stay closed, for privacy. Besides, she liked the feeling of being cocooned in such close quarters with Adam, insulated from the outside world by the steamy glass. They were going to be late for their meeting, but inside this cloud, she didn't care.

'We should go in,' she said half-heartedly.

'Just five more minutes. It's not like they can start without you.'

Right, Cassie thought, because I'm a leader. All the more reason not to be late because I'm making out with my boyfriend.

Boyfriend. The notion still made her giddy, even after all these weeks. She watched the way the setting sun brought out the multicoloured highlights in Adam's tangled hair – shades of burgundy and orange – and the crystalline sparkle in his blue eyes.

He leaned in and softly kissed the spot on the side of her neck just below her ear. 'Fine,' she said. 'Three more minutes.'

Their first kiss as a couple had changed everything for Cassie. It meant something. Adam's lips on hers felt deliberate and momentous, like an agreement, and her whole body became aware of that fact. This was love, she'd realised.

She assumed the sensation would lessen as the days passed, that their kissing would become routine and habitual, but it hadn't. If anything, its intensity increased over time. Parked now just outside the old lighthouse on Shore Road, Cassie knew they had to stop kissing, but she couldn't. And neither could Adam. The quickening of his breath and the pressing urgency of his grip on her hips made that obvious.

But it wouldn't look good to walk in late to her first meeting as a Circle leader. 'We really have to go in,' she said, pulling away and placing her hand against Adam's chest to hold him still.

He took a deep breath and exhaled through his mouth, trying to cool himself down. 'I know.'

Reluctantly, he let Cassie disentangle from his embrace and make herself more presentable. After a few more deep breaths, and a swift patting down of his wild hair, he followed her inside.

Walking across the long-grassed meadow that led to the old lighthouse, Cassie couldn't help but be struck by its worn, rustic beauty. Melanie had told them it dated back to the late 1700s, and its age was evident in its dilapidated appearance. The tower itself was constructed of greyed stone and brick reaching almost ninety feet high, but at its base was a small, crumbling wooden house – the lightkeeper's cottage. It had been built for the lightkeeper's wife and children, so they could be close to him while he saw to his duties upstairs. According to Melanie, the cottage was passed down through several generations until the lighthouse was finally decommissioned in the early 1900s. Since then, there had been talk of converting it into a museum, but it had remained abandoned for decades.

Adam smiled at her, and her breath caught in her throat. She unlatched the cottage door and stepped inside, Adam just behind her. With an almost audible whoosh, the Circle's focus shifted to her grand, belated entrance.

It was immediately obvious that they'd kept the group waiting for too long. And that the group knew exactly what she and Adam had been doing. Cassie examined their faces, absorbing their different reactions and silent accusations.

Melanie's usually cool eyes contained a heated impatience, and Laurel shyly giggled. Deborah, sitting on the edge of the wooden bench in the corner, appeared ready to make a snide comment, but before she had the chance, Chris and Doug Henderson, who'd been playing catch with a tennis ball by the window, said in unison, 'Well, it's about frigging time.'

Nick, sitting on the floor with his back against the wall, looked at Cassie with a subtle pain in his eyes that forced her to turn away.

'Adam,' Faye said in her lazy, husky voice, 'your lip gloss is smudged.'

The room broke out in uncontrollable laughter, and Adam's face reddened. Diana stared straight down at the floor, humiliated for them, or perhaps for herself. She'd been gracious about Adam being with Cassie now, but there was only so much a girl could take.

'We call this meeting to order,' Diana said, regaining her poise. 'Everyone, please be seated.'

Diana spoke as if the laughter had died down, but it was still loud and raucous. 'The first order of business,' she continued, 'is what we're going to do with the Master Tools.'

That quieted the group. The Master Tools — the

diadem, the silver bracelet, and the leather garter – had belonged to Black John's original coven. They'd been hidden for hundreds of years until Cassie figured out they were concealed within the fireplace in her grandmother's kitchen. The Circle had used the Tools to defeat Black John, but they'd put off making any decisions regarding them since. Tonight, the time had come to determine their fate.

'That's right,' Cassie said, joining Diana in the centre of the room. 'We have real power now. And we need to—'

What? What did they need to do? She turned to Diana. Her green eyes and shining hair were radiant, even in the ghostly lantern light of the old cottage. If anyone knew what the Circle should do next, it was Diana.

'I think we should destroy the power of the Master Tools somehow,' Diana said in her clear, musical voice. 'So no one can use them.'

For a moment, nobody spoke. They were all too shocked by this suggestion. Then Faye broke the silence. 'You've got to be kidding me,' she said. 'You and Adam have spent half your lives trying to find the Master Tools.'

'I know,' Diana said. 'But after all we've been through, and now that we've defeated Black John, I feel like that much power can't be good for us, or for anyone.'

Cassie was as surprised as Faye. These words didn't

sound like Diana at all, or at least not like the Diana she had known.

Adam appeared taken aback as well, but he kept quiet. Leaders spoke first. Those were the rules.

Cassie felt the attention of the group settle on her. They were a triumvirate now, which meant her power was equal to both Diana's and Faye's. She wanted to use her authority well, to state her opinion openly and intelligently, but she didn't want to go against Diana.

'What made you change your mind?' she said.

Diana crossed her thin arms over her chest. 'People change their minds all the time, Cassie.'

'Well,' Faye said, focusing on Diana with her honey-coloured eyes. 'I disagree entirely. It would be a waste not to use the Tools. At the very least we should experiment with them.' Her mouth formed a cruel smile. 'Don't you agree, Cassie?'

'Um,' she said. It was weird. Cassie kind of agreed with Faye on this one, which might have been the first time she ever agreed with Faye on anything. She didn't want to side with Faye over Diana, but how could they just destroy the Tools? What if Black John came back? These were their only means of self-defence. She wished Diana had discussed this with her before now.

'We can talk to Constance about help getting rid of them,'

Diana offered. 'If that's what we decide to do.'

Melanie's great-aunt Constance had been helping the Circle with their magic. Since she'd tapped into her powers to nurse Cassie's mother back to health last winter, she'd become more willing to share her knowledge of the old ways.

'Constance probably knows a spell we can use,' Diana said. 'And with Black John gone for good, I bet she'll agree it's time to put the Tools to rest.'

Cassie could see Diana felt strongly about this. As did Faye – that familiar fiery anger had sneaked its way into her sharp features.

'We should take a vote,' a strong voice called out. It belonged to Nick, who rarely spoke at Circle meetings. Hearing him express an opinion on this caught Cassie off guard.

'Nick's right,' Melanie said. 'We should all have equal say in a decision this important.'

Diana nodded. 'I'm fine with that.'

Faye dramatically swept her red nails at the group. 'Vote then,' she said with the confidence of someone who'd already won.

Melanie stood and stepped to the centre of the room. She always called out Circle votes, Cassie noticed. 'All those in favour of destroying the Master Tools,' she said, 'raise your hands.'

Diana's hand went up first, followed by Melanie's own, then Laurel's. After a second-long pause, Nick raised his, and then finally Adam.

Cassie couldn't believe it. Adam had voted with Diana even though she knew he'd rather experiment with the Tools.

'All those in favour of keeping the Tools,' Melanie said, 'raise your—'

'Wait,' Cassie called out. She'd become distracted and lost the chance to choose Diana's side.

Faye laughed. 'You snooze, you lose, Cassie. And a vote against Diana is a vote for me.'

'Wrong,' Cassie said, surprising herself as she said it. 'It's a vote for me.'

She paused to look at Adam and saw he was smiling proudly.

'I propose a third option,' she said. 'We keep the Tools, in case we need them. We don't destroy their power, but we also don't experiment with them.'

'In that case,' Faye said, 'I'd be happy to keep the Tools safe until we need them.'

'Not a chance,' Adam said.

Cassie raised her hand. 'I wasn't finished.' She eyed Faye and then Diana. 'I propose that each leader hides one of the three relics, so they can only be used if the whole group knows about it.'

Everyone became quiet then, as they mulled this new possibility over in their minds.

It was a good idea, and Cassie knew it. What she didn't know was how she'd come up with it right there on the spot like that. When she took control of the floor, she hadn't had the slightest idea what she was going to say.

Diana spoke first. 'That does seem like a fair compromise,' she said. 'Melanie, I call for a revote.'

'I second the call for a revote,' Nick said gallantly.

Melanie raised her eyebrows. 'Okay then. All those in favour of . . . Cassie's idea, raise your hand.'

All hands went up, except for Deborah's, Suzan's and Faye's.

'It's decided then,' Melanie said.

Faye stood perfectly still. She didn't move a muscle, but a dark shadow fell over her face.

Suzan bounced out of her chair. 'Oh, well,' she said. 'I guess that's that. I'm starving. Can we go and eat now?'

'Yeah, let's go and get tacos,' Sean said.

One by one, everyone stood up and began gathering their things, talking about meeting at Melanie's aunt Constance's later to practise their invocations. Diana snuffed out the candles and turned down the lanterns. All the while, Faye remained motionless.

'You,' she said.

Instinctively, Cassie took a step back, even though Faye was across the room.

'Don't be too proud of yourself.' She sauntered over to Cassie and leaned in close. Cassie could smell her heady perfume and it made her dizzy. 'You might have won the battle,' Faye said. 'But . . . well, you know.'

Cassie drew away from Faye's reach. Her fear still got the best of her every time Faye threatened her. Whether or not Faye was actually stronger was beside the point. She had the singularity of mind of a sociopath and a complete lack of conscience. Faye couldn't be reasoned with, and that was what made her dangerous.

'We're on the same side,' Cassie said weakly. 'We want the same thing.'

Faye narrowed her honey-coloured eyes. 'Not really,' she said. 'Not yet, anyway.'

It sounded like a threat, and Cassie knew Faye never made an empty threat.

If you've got a thirst for
fiction, join up now

bookswithbite.co.uk

Packed with sneak peeks, book trailers, exclusive
competitions and downloads, **bookswithbite.co.uk**
is the new place on the web to get your fix of
great fiction.

Sign up to the newsletter at
www.bookswithbite.co.uk
for the latest news on your favourite authors,
to receive exclusive extra content and the
opportunity to enter special
members-only competitions.

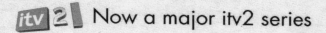

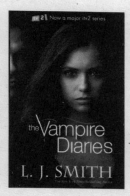

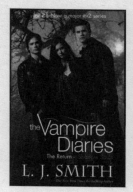
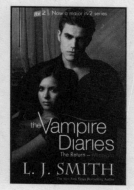

A WITCH in WINTER

When love is tangled up in magic, how can you be sure what's real?

Anna Winterson doesn't know she's a witch and would probably mock you for believing in magic, but after moving to the small town of Winter with her father, she learns more than she ever wanted to about power.

When Anna meets Seth, she is smitten, but when she enchants him to love her, she unwittingly amplifies a deadly conflict between two witch clans and splits her own heart in two …

www.ruthwarburton.com
www.hodderchildrens.co.uk

MIST

The last shred of the mist swirled and drew back, and she saw where she was. She was very, very far from home.

Midnight: a mist-haunted wood with a bad reputation. A sweet sixteen party, and thirteen-year-old Nell is trying to keep her sister, spoilt birthday-girl Gwen, out of trouble. No chance. Trouble finds Gwen and drags her through the mist.

Only Nell guesses who's behind the kidnap - the boy she hoped was her friend, the gorgeous but mysterious Evan River.

Not alive. Not dead. Somewhere in between
lie the Beautiful Dead.

A stunning series that will leave you restless.

Books 1-4
OUT NOW

THE SECRET CIRCLE

THE INITIATION AND THE CAPTIVE PART I

Cassie is not happy about moving from sunny California to gloomy New England. She longs for her old life, her old friends … But when she starts to form a bond with a clique of terrifying but seductive teenagers at her new school, she thinks maybe she could fit in after all …

Initiated into the Secret Circle, she is pulled along by the deadly and intoxicating thrill of this powerful and gifted coven. But then she falls in love, and has a daunting choice to make. She must resist temptation or risk dark forces to get what she wants.

www.bookswithbite.co.uk

Sign up to the mailing list to find out about the latest releases from L. J. Smith

Final Friends

VOLUME ONE

just wanted to finish high school,
igh school might finish them …

n Jessica Hart decides to throw
ty in order to get to know some
e hot new guys at school, she could
r have predicted that by the end
e night someone would be dead …

t people figured it was suicide …
figured wrong.

www.bookswithbite.co.uk

un to the mailing list to find out about the latest releases from Christopher P